A CALL OF LOVE

Then, as Aisha pulled back the curtain to place the hanger onto the rail, she gave a scream of horror.

Hiding behind the curtain was Arthur Watkins!

He stepped out smiling and crowed,

"You thought you were free of me, pretty lady, but I don't give up so easily."

As he spoke, he seized her arm.

Then he placed one hand over her mouth so that she could not scream again.

Arthur Watkins had actually been thinking all day of how he could be in touch with what he had decided was the prettiest girl he had ever seen.

He had always moved in a Society where money was much more important than breeding or education and, because he was so rich, he was used to having any interest he showed in a woman reciprocated.

Because Aisha had avoided him, she had set him a challenge and a challenge was something that he had never refused or ignored in his busy and successful life.

THE BARBARA CARTLAND PINK COLLECTION

Titles in this series

A CALL OF LOVE

BARBARA CARTLAND

Barbaracartland.com Ltd

THE BARBARA CARTLAND PINK COLLECTION

Dame Barbara Cartland is still regarded as the most prolific bestselling author in the history of the world.

In her lifetime she was frequently in the Guinness Book of Records for writing more books than any other living author.

Her most amazing literary feat was to double her output from 10 books a year to over 20 books a year when she was 77 to meet the huge demand.

She went on writing continuously at this rate for 20 years and wrote her very last book at the age of 97, thus completing an incredible 400 books between the ages of 77 and 97.

Her publishers finally could not keep up with this phenomenal output, so at her death in 2000 she left behind an amazing 160 unpublished manuscripts, something that no other author has ever achieved.

Barbara's son, Ian McCorquodale, together with his daughter Iona, felt that it was their sacred duty to publish all these titles for Barbara's millions of admirers all over the world who so love her wonderful romances.

So in 2004 they started publishing the 160 brand new Barbara Cartlands as *The Barbara Cartland Pink Collection*, as Barbara's favourite colour was always pink – and yet more pink!

The Barbara Cartland Pink Collection is published monthly exclusively by Barbaracartland.com and the books are numbered in sequence from 1 to 160.

Enjoy receiving a brand new Barbara Cartland book each month by taking out an annual subscription to the Pink Collection, or purchase the books individually.

The Pink Collection is available from the Barbara Cartland website www.barbaracartland.com via mail order and through all good bookshops.

In addition Ian and Iona are proud to announce that The Barbara Cartland Pink Collection is now available in ebook format as from Valentine's Day 2011.

For more information, please contact us at:

Barbaracartland.com Ltd.
Camfield Place
Hatfield
Hertfordshire AL9 6JE
United Kingdom

Telephone: +44 (0)1707 642629
Fax: +44 (0)1707 663041
Email: info@barbaracartland.com

THE LATE DAME BARBARA CARTLAND

Barbara Cartland who sadly died in May 2000 at the age of nearly 99 was the world's most famous romantic novelist who wrote 723 books in her lifetime with worldwide sales of over 1 billion copies and her books were translated into 36 different languages.

As well as romantic novels, she wrote historical biographies, 6 autobiographies, theatrical plays, books of advice on life, love, vitamins and cookery. She also found time to be a political speaker and television and radio personality.

She wrote her first book at the age of 21 and this was called *Jigsaw*. It became an immediate bestseller and sold 100,000 copies in hardback and was translated into 6 different languages. She wrote continuously throughout her life, writing bestsellers for an astonishing 76 years. Her books have always been immensely popular in the United States, where in 1976 her current books were at numbers 1 & 2 in the B. Dalton bestsellers list, a feat never achieved before or since by any author.

Barbara Cartland became a legend in her own lifetime and will be best remembered for her wonderful romantic novels, so loved by her millions of readers throughout the world.

Her books will always be treasured for their moral message, her pure and innocent heroines, her good looking and dashing heroes and above all her belief that the power of love is more important than anything else in everyone's life.

"If you really love someone, you are a part of him and he is a part of you. You know what he is thinking, you know what he is feeling and above all you know that he loves you, as indeed you love him."

Barbara Cartland

CHAPTER ONE
1880

Lord Kenington woke with a start and remembered that he was at sea.

He had been very tired when he came aboard the P & O Liner, which was taking him to India.

After eating a supper brought to his cabin by his valet, he had climbed into bed. He knew that he had a great deal to think about and decide on when he was alone, but instead he had fallen asleep.

Now, as he glanced at the clock beside him, he saw that it was well into a new day.

He had been extremely busy before he had come on board.

The Prime Minister had asked him if he would go out to India and bring back to him a personal report on the situation on the frontier of that country.

India was of huge importance to Great Britain and there was an unmistakable menace from the Russians.

The Cossacks, riding magnificently across Southern Asia, were coming nearer and nearer to what was always considered the brightest jewel in the British Crown.

Queen Victoria herself had told Lord Kenington that she wanted a much more intimate report than she had been currently receiving and the Prime Minister had spent several hours discussing his mission with him.

Now, having rung for his valet, Lord Kenington got up and began to dress, having decided that he would go down to breakfast rather than have it in his cabin.

He had made it a rule never to talk while he was dressing. He always disliked chatter early in the morning and his valet therefore handed him his clothes one by one without saying a word.

Then he walked out and onto the deck for a little fresh air before he went to the Saloon for breakfast.

They were a long way down the English Channel and he realised they would soon be in the Bay of Biscay, which was invariably rough however bright the sunshine.

As he was an excellent sailor, a rough sea did not worry him, in fact he rather enjoyed it.

As he walked round the deck, he thought by the time he reached India he would be sadly short of exercise.

In London he would normally ride his exceedingly fine horses in Rotten Row early in the morning and, when he was in the country, he had an early breakfast so that he could ride for at least two hours before he started work.

He should, at the age of twenty-eight, have been enjoying himself, like most of his friends, with the beauties in Mayfair who were hotly pursued by the Prince of Wales.

Lord Kenington had, however, found recently that however beautiful a woman might be, in a short while she became boring.

Although it might seem absurd, he really preferred working to making love.

This suited the Prime Minister and the Secretary of State for Foreign Affairs, who both regularly consulted him on various matters of State. If there was trouble in Paris, it was said almost automatically,

"Oh, send Kenington over to see what is wrong," and then the Prime Minister would insist that the same rule applied to most other countries in Europe.

He had inherited his brain and air of authority from a long line of impressive ancestors, who had played their part in English politics from the moment they were born.

When Lord Kenington's father died and he came into the title, there was no doubt that young Charles was a 'chip off the old block'.

At Eton he had always been top of the class and at Cambridge University he had been awarded a First.

"The trouble with you, Charles, is that you have too many brains for your age," one of his friends said to him. "You make us all feel stupid and we naturally resent it."

Lord Kenington had smiled, but did not reply and he knew only too well that his friends would be more than willing to accept his many invitations to shoot, to hunt and to take part in the steeplechase that was one of the great events in the spring.

At his home, which was one of the finest ancestral houses in the whole of England, everything ran perfectly like clockwork.

He was not required to give very much personal attention to it and this left him free for the political and diplomatic world in which he had made his name.

Invariably he was involved in every crisis, whether it happened in London, Europe or Timbuktu.

His mother had been delighted when he told her that he was going to India.

"Whether you like it or not, dearest Charles," she said, "you will have a rest on the way out and on the way back for at least seventeen days each way. That is what I have been wanting for you for some time."

3

"Wanting for me, but why Mama?" he had asked. "You are not suggesting that I am not in good health?"

"I still think you are spending far too much time in so many consultations and private meetings," she replied. "I am looking for the day when you bring home a wife and then have at least three sons to inherit your name and your glorious homes."

Lord Kenington had thrown up his hands,

"Oh, not that again, Mama!" he complained. "I am sick to death of being told I should marry and settle down! As you well know, if I did so, I would be bored to tears and would probably leave my wife at home and go round the world on my own."

His mother had laughed, but at the same time there was an anxious expression in her eyes. She felt, as mothers often do, that her beloved son, and he was the only one, was wasting his youth.

He was so handsome that it seemed absurd that he was shut up day after day with men old enough to be his father on matters she felt they should know better than he.

Now there was trouble in India, but as his mother had said plaintively,

"There is always trouble there. I cannot think why they cannot solve it themselves without you having to be called in."

"It is a compliment, Mama. In fact I would have been hurt and surprised if they had not asked my opinion."

There was nothing his mother could say except to beg him to rest when he had the chance.

He must not wear himself out over troubles which, as everybody knew, were inevitable, as the British Empire expanded more and more every day.

However Lord Kenington had set off optimistically.

He was determined to solve all the problems that awaited him and yet, as his mother had foretold, he was glad of the rest he would be obliged to take on the voyage.

He said to himself as he drove to Tilbury,

'At least I will have a chance to read.'

He devoured books, his mother said, in the way that a hungry animal devours its food and he had put a pile on one side for his valet to pack with his clothes.

Now, as he had walked round the deck for the third time, he thought he should go into breakfast and he would then see what his fellow passengers were like.

He had been invited to sit at the Captain's table, which was a compliment, but he had managed to refuse by saying he had so much work to do and he might therefore be erratic in the times he came into meals.

So he had been given a table to himself on one side of the dining room and he then had a good view of the other passengers from where he was sitting.

They were, he realised at once, very much what he had expected.

They were all First Class passengers, including a number of Officers returning from leave, also Subalterns going out for the first time and excited at being sent to the East. There were inevitably a good number of middle-aged couples and large women who talked too loudly and were somewhat over-dressed.

The breakfast was reasonable, but not particularly imaginative and he did not waste much time over it.

When he rose from his table, one of the Stewards hurried to open the door for him and he thanked him as he walked out.

He had intended to go back to his cabin to collect a book he was reading and take it on deck.

But, as he passed the library, he thought it would be a good idea to see if there was anything he liked the look of before the rest of the passengers took the best books away.

He turned and went into the library, which was no more than a small cabin.

It was well stocked with books, even though they were not the sort that he would be likely to read. A large number were novels and there was a shelf of guide books.

These were particularly popular with people going to the East, who had not brought one themselves and so they read them avidly from cover to cover. And, as this ship was a new one, the books were new too.

Lord Kenington thought there might conceivably be a book on India he had not read, although he had ordered his secretary to purchase all those that had been recently published.

He was looking along a shelf in the library, when a voice beside him said,

"Please can I talk to you, my Lord?"

Lord Kenington looked round and saw that there was a young woman standing beside him.

At a first glance he thought she was very pretty, but he realised from the expression in her eyes and the way she spoke that for some reason she was fearful.

"Yes, of course," he replied. "And what can I do for you?"

"It is just," she said in a voice that shook a little, "that – I want to be seen talking to you. As you – are so important, my Lord, perhaps it will make the man – who is frightening me go away."

"Frightening you? Why should he do that?"

The girl, for she was obviously quite young, looked over her shoulder and, as there was no one in the library or as far as she could see outside, she answered,

"He has been pestering me ever since I came on board and I was very scared last night."

She paused for a moment and, as Lord Kenington did not speak, she went on,

"When I saw you at breakfast, I thought, as you are so well known that if he saw me speaking to you, he would perhaps – keep away from me."

The words seemed to just fall from her lips and he realised that she really was very frightened.

"Let's go out on deck," he suggested. "Then you can tell me about this man. This place is so small that, if we talk in here, anyone who comes in is bound to overhear what we are saying."

"That is most kind of you. I knew, because I read about you in the newspapers, that you are so distinguished that anyone would be afraid to annoy you in any way."

Lord Kenington smiled.

"I wish that was true. So let's find a place to sit where we will not be disturbed."

They went out on deck and he found a place that was sheltered from the wind and, once they were sitting down, no one could sit near to them.

He felt, as he looked at her, that she was obviously a lady and that she was even prettier than he had thought her to be when she first spoke to him.

"Now tell me," he began, "what all this is about."

As she drew in her breath, he added,

"Surely you are not travelling alone? Is there not someone chaperoning you?"

"It was all arranged," she said, "that I should be looked after by the Dean of Worcester and his wife who were going to India. But unfortunately he was taken ill at the last moment and they had to cancel their journey."

"So you came alone. That was not very wise."

"I know, my Lord, but I was so anxious to get out to Papa and I did not think anyone would take any notice of me."

As she spoke, she looked round, almost as if she expected the man to be standing nearby and watching her.

"Then what happened?" Lord Kenington enquired.

"Last night when I was having dinner alone and, as I had stupidly refused to go to the Captain's table, he came to sit down beside me and started to talk. I thought he was very pushy and I said very little. But afterwards he insisted on taking me out on deck. Then he became familiar."

She stopped and he saw the colour come into her cheeks.

"I suppose you are saying," he said quietly, "that he tried to kiss you."

"He tried – but I ran away," the girl replied, "and locked myself in my cabin."

"That was sensible," Lord Kenington murmured.

"Yes, but he found out where I was sleeping and knocked on the door. He made such a noise that some of the nearby passengers complained and this morning I had to apologise to them."

"So you thought I would be able to protect you from this man."

"Because you are so important," the girl replied, "I felt, if he saw you talking to me, he would keep away."

"You cannot be sure of that. I suggest you tell me what your name is and if you know the name of this man who is being so tiresome."

"I am sorry, my Lord. I should have introduced myself when I was brave enough to speak to you."

"Well, you can be brave again now," he smiled.

"My name is Aisha Warde, and my father is Major Harold Warde, who is serving in India at the moment."

Lord Kenington thought that he had heard of him or had read the name somewhere, but he did not have any clear idea of who he was and therefore did not interrupt.

"It is very exciting for me to go out to India to be with Papa," Aisha was saying, "and I could not bear to tell him at the last moment that I could not come because I did not have a chaperone."

"I can understand that and, of course, this man who is troubling you must be told to behave. Do you know his name?"

"He told me that his name is Arthur Watkins, but I don't think he is a gentleman or anywhere near it."

"He most certainly does not sound like one," Lord Kenington replied. "I will see that he does not upset you again."

"Will you really do so, my Lord? It is very kind of you."

"I still think it rather dangerous for you to be travelling alone with no one to chaperone you. I will make enquiries from the Purser to see if there may be people on board who would be glad for you to have meals with them and, of course, to see that no one knocks on your door in that unpleasant fashion."

"It was most alarming. In fact I was afraid the lock might give way and the door fly open."

"I think, as this is a new ship that the locks will be strong enough to resist any intruders, whether they are after your money or you."

Aisha laughed as he had intended and then she said,

"It is very kind of you to take so much trouble, my Lord. I am only sorry to be a nuisance."

"You are nothing of the sort. I am travelling alone and, when I looked round at the rest of the passengers this morning, I decided I had no wish to talk to any of them!"

Aisha giggled.

"I felt the same. Then this horrible man came to sit at my table and I could not send him away."

"I think you were rather unwise not to sit with the Captain as you should have done."

"I thought the people at his table would want to talk to me and I had seen that some of them are rather strange-looking men who were obviously travelling alone."

Lord Kenington thought that she was rather more intelligent than the average young girl.

She was clearly well aware that a man travelling on his own might be looking for someone as young and pretty as she was to pass the time with.

"I will speak to the Purser," he said, "and see that this does not happen to you again. Will you come with me or will you wait here until I come back?"

"You will come back?" Aisha asked and now her voice was sounding anxious again.

"Yes, I will come back," Lord Kenington promised.

He walked to the Purser's office, which was not far, and, when he entered, he was instantly bowed to and the Purser enquired if there was anything he could do for him.

"I have just been talking to a young lady passenger on board called Miss Warde, who I understand is having trouble from one of the passengers."

"Trouble, my Lord?" the Purser enquired sharply.

"Yes, a man called Arthur Watkins is pestering her as she is travelling alone."

"Did you say Mr. Arthur Watkins, my Lord?"

"Yes, that is the name. And I think that you should reprimand him sharply for upsetting a young girl and tell him to behave himself. In fact I am surprised he is in First Class."

Lord Kenington spoke in an authoritative voice and then he realised that the Purser was looking rather worried.

"What is the matter?" he asked. "Surely you can speak to the man."

"It will be very difficult for me to do so, my Lord."

"Why?"

"Mr. Watkins is one of our big shareholders and we have been told that when he travels to make sure that he has every possible comfort and attention."

"Are you certain we are speaking about the same man?" Lord Kenington asked.

"As far as we are concerned, my Lord, there is only one Arthur Watkins aboard and he is in the best cabin. In fact, as we don't have sitting rooms, the cabin next to his cabin is always kept for him, so he can entertain privately anyone he wishes."

Lord Kenington was sure an invitation to that cabin would soon be given to Aisha.

So he therefore remarked,

"I understand your difficulty. At the same time the young lady who has complained to me is unfortunately travelling without a chaperone. So she is frightened by the way Mr. Watkins is behaving."

The Purser scratched his head.

"I could change Miss Warde into a different cabin," he said, "but I doubt if it would remain unknown to Mr. Watkins. He only has to look at the list over here, which of

11

course he is entitled to do, to learn exactly where everyone is sleeping."

"As Miss Warde has applied to me for help," Lord Kenington replied, "perhaps there is an unoccupied cabin near me where I could keep an eye on her. I think I know her father and it would be extremely regrettable if she was frightened or upset because, through no fault of her own, she was travelling without a chaperone."

The Purser put his Register down on the table so that Lord Kenington could examine it.

"There's an empty cabin next to yours, my Lord," he said, "but I was, in fact, keeping it for a passenger who is coming aboard at Gibraltar."

"Then maybe this passenger could be put elsewhere or in the cabin now occupied by Miss Warde."

He knew that if he had been anyone else, the Purser would have insisted that the cabin next to his was too good for a young girl and it should therefore be reserved for the distinguished personage embarking at Gibraltar.

Equally he was well aware that there was no one else on board who could equal his own prominence.

So he was not surprised that the Purser was not prepared to argue the matter with him on the subject

"Very well, my Lord. I'll now tell the Stewardess to move Miss Warde's belongings into the cabin next to yours. If you're sure that Miss Warde can pay the extra price that we charge for our best cabins."

"Thank you and see that it is done immediately. I will tell Miss Warde how accommodating you have been and I am sure that she will be very grateful."

He walked away, not aware that the Purser had turned to his assistant to say,

"Here's a pretty mess to say the least. If Watkins knows I'm interfering with what he thinks is his fun, he'll kick up a right row at Headquarters and I'll be the one for the high jump!"

The Assistant Purser looked round to make sure he was not overheard before he replied,

"Money or no money, Watkins is an unpleasant bit of work, as well you know."

Lord Kenington had now gone back to where Aisha was waiting for him.

When he reached her, she jumped up and asked,

"Have you been able to move me, my Lord, or is the ship too full?"

"I have been able to move you," he replied.

She gave a cry of relief,

"Oh, how kind of you, but do you think he will find out where I have gone? The Purser may tell him."

"You are being moved into the cabin next to mine and I think you can trust me to deal with any man who behaves in such an offensive manner. As a matter of fact I understand he is a big shareholder in the P & O Company."

Aisha gave a cry of horror.

"In which case, he probably feels he owns the ship and may refuse to allow me to be moved."

"I think however rich he may be," Lord Kenington said, "he will not wish to quarrel with me."

"No, of course I had forgotten for a moment how important you are. Your name is in all the newspapers day after day and I have often wondered what you were like."

Lord Kenington smiled.

"What am I like?"

"The kindest and most helpful man that I have ever known. You might easily have thought I was very forward to ask for your help. But I knew instinctively you were the only person who could assist me. Papa always says, 'never be afraid of doing what is right'."

"I see that your father gives you excellent advice."

"I only hope he is taking care of himself," Aisha replied. "As perhaps you know, he goes on very difficult and dangerous missions, so naturally I worry about him."

Lord Kenington remembered now where he had heard about Major Warde.

He was one of the people who had been active in starting what was known as *The Great Game*. It was one of the extraordinary organisations that had been created recently.

He knew, as only a very few others knew, that the authorities in India were greatly worried by the infiltration of the Russians into Asia.

The Cossacks, riding fast horses and taking their victims by surprise, had advanced considerably in the last two or three years and they were now uncomfortably near to the frontiers of India.

It had all begun in the early years of the nineteenth century, when Russian troops had started to find their way Southwards through the Caucasus, then inhabited by fierce Muslim tribesmen, towards Northern Persia.

At the start, like Russian's great march Eastwards towards Siberia two centuries earlier, this did not seem to pose any particular threat to British interests.

No one took Russia too seriously in those days and their nearest frontier posts were too far distant to threaten any danger to the British East India Company's territory.

Then, as Lord Kenington knew, in the early 1800s intelligence reached London that was to cause considerable alarm, both to the British Government and to the East India Company's Directors.

Many politicians, especially the authorities in India, were now certain that the Russians intended to try to wrest India from Britain.

And that was the reason why Lord Kenington was going to India.

"I want to know what you think they are planning to do," the Prime Minister had said. "And whether, if a Russian force did reach India after overcoming all the obstacles on the way, we would be strong enough to drive them back."

The Prime Minister was talking to Lord Kenington alone, as he was well aware that there were members of the Cabinet who thought that he was being hysterical and that it would be impossible for Russia to withstand the British Army if they were forced into a man to man fight.

But Mr. Benjamin Disraeli, the Prime Minister, was undoubtedly troubled.

When he sent Lord Kenington to India he had said,

"I want to find out the truth, the whole truth and nothing but the truth. I know that is what you will bring me back, however incredible it may seem to some of the people here who never wish to face up to these matters of urgency until it is too late."

There had been a scathing note in his voice as he spoke the last words and Lord Kenington was well aware that he was having trouble with his Cabinet. There were those who did not wish to spend too much money or send too many good men out to India.

He promised the Prime Minister that he would find out the truth, but he could not help wondering whether it was possible here and now to anticipate what might happen in the next ten or twenty years.

He had therefore brought with him a great number of books and he hoped they would tell him more about India than he knew at the moment.

And he had certainly not expected his voyage to be interrupted by an extremely pretty and frightened young woman.

He could not tell her that she must fight her own battles and that he could not be involved in them.

He felt that her fear was well-founded, just as he knew the type of man Arthur Watkins was – a girl as pretty as Aisha and travelling alone was an irresistible attraction to a man like him.

'I suppose I will have to take care of her,' he said to himself.

As they sat down side by side, he saw an expression of gratitude in her eyes and yet he knew that he had had no choice in the matter.

"Tell me exactly what you have done, please tell me, my Lord?" Aisha asked with a sense of urgency.

"I have told the Purser to move your things into the cabin next to mine. If that man comes hammering on your door, I will hear him and I will tell him, which is difficult for the Purser to do, to behave himself."

"Have you really done that?" Aisha asked wide-eyed. "How very kind it is of you! I knew when I saw you that you would not fail me and I am sure that he will be too frightened to make a noise outside your cabin."

"There is no need for you to worry any more about it and I think it would be wise if you had your meals either at the Captain's table or with me."

"Of course I would much rather be with you, my Lord. As it happens, Mr. Watkins is sitting at the Captain's table and I am sure he would move into the seat next to me."

She gave a little shudder before she added,

"Last night when he had sat down opposite me, he looked at me in the most horrible manner. I thought, when I hurried away immediately after dinner that I would be free of him. But he came and hammered on my door and I was very very frightened."

"I am sure you were, Aisha. "But I promise you that will not happen tonight. Now I need some exercise. Are you going to stay here or will you walk round the deck with me?"

"If you are quite certain I will not be any trouble, I would love to walk with you. I am too nervous after what happened to walk alone."

"You must of course exercise your legs, as I intend to exercise mine. Therefore let's walk together."

"Thank you! Thank you!" Aisha cried. "I promise not to talk if you prefer to be silent. Papa has always said I am a very good listener."

"Then you will listen to me when we have our meals together, but now let's concentrate on exercising our legs while the deck is comparatively clear and the waves are not splashing over to make it slippery."

"Do you think that is what will happen when we go through the Bay of Biscay?" Aisha asked.

"I am afraid so, but it's calm in the Mediterranean."

"I am so looking forward to seeing it all. Papa told me in his letters how beautiful the Mediterranean looked on his way to India. Now I am going to see it for myself, just as I will see India instead of only reading about it."

"Is that what you have been doing Aisha?"

"Of course. It's no use going to a place unless you learn first everything you possibly can about it. Although Papa has told me quite a lot, I know there is an enormous amount for me to learn. I have brought two books with me which I hope will tell me a great deal about subjects I am ignorant of at the moment."

"I have quite a number of books with me which I am sure would interest you," Lord Kenington suggested.

Aisha gave a little cry of pleasure.

"If you lend them to me, I promise to be very very careful with them. It's difficult, living in the country, to find all the books one wants to read and I was hoping that the Dean, who was coming to India, would have a small library with him, as it would be a new life that he has never lived before."

Lord Kenington laughed.

"Most people," he said, "are content with what they see and hear and don't investigate any further. But I feel that you are doing the right thing, which is learning about India from the many good books written on the subject."

"Some of which you have with you," Aisha added, "and thank you, thank you for saying I may read them."

It passed through Lord Kenington's mind that the average girl did not read anything at all serious. Those he had talked to, who had been pressed on him by ambitious mothers, had usually read nothing, except maybe the latest novel or more likely the social pages of the newspapers.

He thought that Aisha was certainly different and, if her father was the man he was thinking about, he too was very different.

He did not wish to ask her any questions at this stage, but he was fairly sure that Major Warde was one of the people he had hoped to meet when he reached India.

He was wise enough not to follow to the letter the Prime Minister's instructions and he intended to consult the Viceroy and members of his staff about the position and also to talk to the men who had conceived and put into action *The Great Game*.

It was, he had learnt, run by a number of Army Officers and some Indians who had no wish to be trampled on by the Russians.

'I will know much more when I reach India,' Lord Kenington said to himself.

At the same time he could not help thinking that by befriending Aisha Warde he would gain the gratitude and confidence of her father and Major Warde, unless he was mistaken, would be an extremely important contact.

*

He and Aisha spent the rest of the afternoon reading comfortably in the sunshine.

Then they went to change for dinner.

Aisha was ready well before the time that Lord Kenington said they would go to the Saloon together.

She left her cabin to take back to the library the book she had borrowed when she came aboard.

When she looked at it more closely, she had found it was badly written. The only merit it had was that the illustrations in it were fairly good.

Now she had the choice of the books belonging to Lord Kenington she had no further use for this book and she thought she would put it back on the shelf from where she had taken it.

She walked into the library and, as there was no one there, she went straight to the shelf and put back the book.

Then, as she turned round, she saw with a jerk of horror that Arthur Watkins was standing in the doorway, watching her.

He was a very unprepossessing man of over forty. His hair was already growing thin and there were lines on his face that were clear signs of debauchery.

Equally he was very sure of himself because he was so rich and he had in fact made a fortune where other men had failed dismally.

He found pretty young girls irresistible and he spent a great deal of time and money on them.

When he saw Aisha coming aboard, he had thought that she was quite the loveliest girl he had seen for a long time and he had therefore hoped to enjoy the voyage far more than he had expected.

And so he was determined not to be frustrated.

It was sheer willpower that had raised him from what was almost the gutter to the position he was now in and he had, as flatterers told him, reached when he was not yet forty, a position most men would have given their eyes to hold.

'I am clever, and no man, and certainly no woman, can get the better of me,' he had often said to himself.

He was supremely confident that long before they reached Calcutta he would have taken possession of the very pretty and attractive young woman who was climbing the gangway just ahead of him.

That she was alone, yet travelling First Class, was a pleasant surprise and, as Arthur Watkins told himself, that would make things very much easier than they might have been otherwise.

He had therefore, at the first opportunity after the ship had moved out of Port, spoken to Aisha, who had answered him politely, as she had obviously been brought up not to be rude to anyone.

He had asked her whether she was going to India and whether she had visited the country before. Then she had slipped away from him to her own cabin before he realised what she was doing.

When he had seen her at dinner, he had thought again that she was exceptionally attractive.

Because he was so rich and because he lived in a very different world from Aisha, it did not occur to him that she would not succumb to his desires and appreciate the amount of money he was prepared to spend on her.

If she was too grand to associate with someone who had started life as an errand boy, she would certainly have a chaperone accompanying her on the voyage.

When dinner was over, Aisha quite innocently had gone on deck, as she wanted to see the moon rising up into the sky and the stars reflected on the sea.

When Arthur Watkins had joined her, she had not at first been alarmed. He had asked her name and she had told it to him.

The music played by the band and the moonlight made the night seem very romantic.

It was then that Aisha realised that Arthur Watkins was putting his arm round her and she woke up to reality and gave a cry of protest.

"Now don't be afraid of me," Arthur Watkins said in his rather common voice. "I think you're very pretty and we'll have a lot of fun together, we will."

He tried to kiss her.

However, she fought herself free and ran away too quickly for him to be able to catch her.

When she reached her cabin, she locked the door and sank down onto the bunk.

She felt her heart was bursting from her breast and her breath was coming quickly from between her lips.

She was very frightened.

No man had ever tried to kiss her before.

She realised, now it was too late, that she had been very stupid to stand talking to a stranger in the moonlight.

'Just how could I have been so foolish?' she asked herself.

She realised that it was because she had never been entirely alone before. There had always been her mother or her Governess or one of her relations.

Now she had seventeen days ahead of her with no one to turn to if that unpleasant man tried once again to kiss her.

It was then, as she began to undress, that there was a knock on the door.

Instinctively she turned to see who it was and then, at the last moment, she had the common sense to ask,

"Who is it?"

"It's me," a man's voice answered. "Now don't be afraid, pretty lady, I'll do you no harm and I don't want you to run away again."

He was speaking in a low voice to keep other people from hearing what he was saying.

Then, as she moved away from the door, having made sure it was locked, he started to speak more loudly.

"Talk to me!" he called out. "Come out here, I want to see you!"

Aisha had not answered and then he began to knock so loudly that people in the adjacent cabins opened their doors to see what was happening.

Finally Aisha realised that he only stopped making such a noise when people protested and a Stewardess spoke to him severely,

"There's people trying to sleep, sir," Aisha heard the Stewardess say, "and it's time you went to bed instead of keeping them awake."

"There's someone I want to say goodnight to," Arthur Watkins replied. "All she has to do is to open the door, then I'll be as quiet as a little mouse."

"I expect the lady inside has gone to sleep," the Stewardess said, "and that's what you should be doing, sir, and the sooner the better."

"Now don't you cheek me, my girl," he replied. "But just for tonight, as there are many nights ahead of us, I'll do what you say. But don't you be asking too much another time."

"Well, all I can say to you, sir," the Stewardess said sharply, determined to have the last word, "is that there'll not be another time, not in this corridor at any rate."

She must have flounced away and a little later she heard Arthur Watkins' footsteps moving down the passage.

It was then she got into bed and said a prayer of thankfulness to God that he had not been able to intrude on her.

But she was scared, very scared.

She wondered frantically what she could do for the rest of the voyage if he persisted in pestering her.

'There must be someone who can help me,' she said to herself frantically.

Then, as if in answer to her prayer, the following morning she had seen Lord Kenington.

She had known who he was because she recognised him from pictures she had seen in the magazines and she had read all about him in the Parliamentary reports that were always featured in the newspapers her father took.

He was often spoken of as being of great value to Mr. Disraeli, the Prime Minister, also as the owner of fine horses, which last year had won the Derby and the Gold Cup at Ascot.

'He is a gentleman,' Aisha told herself.

When she saw him walk into the library, she had known that that was her opportunity to speak to him.

CHAPTER TWO

Aisha was thrilled with her new cabin.

It was very much larger than the one she had been in previously. It had two portholes, which gave her more light both by day and by night.

There was more room to move about in and more storage space for her clothes.

And so, when she sat down to luncheon with Lord Kenington, she thanked him profusely.

"You have been so kind," she said, "and I am so grateful. Of course Papa will willingly pay the difference in the price of my new cabin."

"You must now tell me about your father," Lord Kenington asked, "because I am most interested in him."

She looked at him questioningly and he explained,

"I believe your father is doing vital work in India."

Again there was silence.

"I hoped you would help me," he said, "because I am going to India in order to find out what the situation is as regards the Russian menace. I believe that your father knows a great deal about it."

Aisha's eyes lit up.

"Oh, that is why you are going out to India!" she exclaimed. "So I need not be careful what I say to you."

"I hope that you will be careful, as well as truthful, but you must not stop me from finding out what I need."

He laughed as he added,

"That sounds complicated, but you will know what I mean."

"Of course I do, my Lord, and if you are really going to India on this important mission, then it would be silly if you did not talk to Papa."

"I have every intention of talking to him. So, if you can help me by telling me where to find him and, without doing anything wrong, inform me as to what he is doing at the moment, it will be of tremendous help."

Aisha lowered her voice before she suggested,

"I think it would be wiser if we talked out on deck. I know that no one can overhear us here, but Papa said that some men can read one's lips at a distance. So I always have to be careful what I was saying even if no one could hear."

Lord Kenington was immediately interested.

He thought that it was just his good luck to find someone like her before he reached India and Aisha, he hoped, could tell him some of the things he had been sent out there to discover.

Equally was it really possible that such a young and pretty girl could tell him anything that he did not already know?

Where India was concerned, the answer was very obviously 'yes'.

They ate their luncheon, which was well served and the Stewards tried to provide Lord Kenington with the wine he particularly requested.

He asked Aisha if she would drink with him, but she shook her head.

"I don't really like wine, my Lord, but I would love some fresh lemonade if they could make it for me."

"I am sure they could do so, Aisha."

And one of the Stewards hurried away.

While they were eating, Aisha was aware that Mr. Watkins at the Captain's table had his eyes on her and so she deliberately did not look again in his direction.

But she could not help feeling a bit uncomfortable, because, without turning her head, she was aware that he was staring at her.

Without her saying anything, Lord Kenington knew what was happening.

"Just pretend to yourself he does not exist," he said. "When I dislike a person, I try to think them out of my mind. It's really quite easy to do. It's a mistake to waste valuable time on being upset by nasty people."

"Of course you are right, my Lord, and that is what I am trying to do. But I can feel him staring at me and almost instinctively I want to look his way to see if he is."

"I know exactly what you mean, because I have felt like that myself. There was a boy at school who I always felt had his eye on me, even when I was sure he was not thinking about me."

"I want to forget that horrible man," Aisha said with a little shiver.

"Just decide he is nothing to do with you and that you are going to forget him."

"That is easier said than done, my Lord."

"Of course it is, but at least you can try."

Because he knew that she was worried by Watkins, Lord Kenington ate quickly and they left the Saloon before anyone else had finished.

They went out onto the deck and sat down at a place that Lord Kenington had found which was protected from the wind and too much sun and it was impossible for anyone to be near them without their being aware of it.

"Now," he said, "tell me about your father, because I really am tremendously interested in him."

"I am sure Papa would be very flattered and I will, of course, tell you everything you want to know, but I have always been afraid that since he takes such tremendous risks, he will be hurt or perhaps killed."

"What risks does he take?" Lord Kenington asked, as Aisha glanced round to make sure that no one was there.

"He is in *The Great Game*. Have you heard about it, my Lord?"

"Indeed I have and I think it is extraordinarily brave of those who take part in it, but I expect your father has told you it is the only way we can find out for sure what is happening on the frontier and how threatening the Russians really are."

"Papa believes that they are very dangerous," Aisha answered, "and, because he speaks Urdu like a native, he often goes – disguised as an Indian."

She almost whispered the last words.

"He goes out amongst the tribes on the North-West Frontier and talks to them?

"He is usually, he told me, dressed as a Holy Man or as an Indian from another part of the country."

Aisha crossed her fingers as she added,

"So far his disguise has never been discovered."

Lord Kenington knew that if it had, he would most probably have lost his life, but, as he had no wish for Aisha to be nervous or unhappy, he said,

"I think that is wonderful of him. How did he learn to speak Urdu so well that no one suspects that he is not an Indian?"

"When he was a small boy, his father was a Judge in India," Aisha replied. "He went to a school where there were Indian boys as well as the sons of English Officers and he has often said that he found the Indians far more interesting and not so unfriendly as the English!"

"So now he is able to disguise himself as an Indian without being noticed."

"I expect, although Papa will never admit it," Aisha said, "that sometimes he is afraid. He went over the North-West Frontier last year and he told me that working outside was most interesting, although somewhat nerve-wracking."

"I am sure. Tell me where your father is now."

"He knows I am arriving on this ship and I expect he will be on the quay at Calcutta waiting for me."

Lord Kenington was delighted, as he had thought it would be difficult to find the men who were on the very secret list of those he should try to contact and that he should meet with Major Warde so quickly would save him a great deal of time and worry.

"I think the luckiest thing that has ever happened to me," he said aloud, "is that you asked me for my help and protection."

"It was very fortunate for me. I slept so peacefully last night, but I know if I had been in my other cabin, it would have been impossible to go to sleep."

"You are not to worry anymore," Lord Kenington said. "I am taking you under my wing, as you might say, and I am quite certain that Mr. Watkins is far too sensible to risk annoying me."

"He is a horrid, beastly man," Aisha insisted, "and I am sure Papa would know how to deal with him. He will be very grateful to you for having saved me as you have."

They sat talking until he said he must take some exercise and they walked round the deck several times.

"When we get to the Mediterranean," he said, "I am sure we will be able to play deck tennis. If you have never played it, I will teach you."

"There is no need to do that," Aisha replied. "I have played before on a short holiday cruise with friends to the Canaries and I won some games even against the men."

"That is certainly a challenge. I will be determined you don't beat me!"

Aisha laughed and then asked him,

"Have you ever in all your life had to accept an inferior position? Have you not always sat on the top of the tree?"

"I suppose if I am honest I should say I have always sat on the top of the tree. Although I must admit to being bullied a certain amount at Eton as they said I was cocky."

"I am sure they would think that still, because you look so superior to everyone else around you."

"Is that really the impression I give?"

Aisha nodded her head.

"Yes it is, and I think perhaps your friends as well as your enemies are somewhat afraid of you."

She saw the surprise on his face and said quickly,

"Please forgive me. I should not have said that. I have been talking to you in the same way as I talk to Papa. He has always said, 'tell the truth and shame the Devil and say exactly what is in your mind. If people don't like it, they need not listen'."

Lord Kenington chuckled.

"That's certainly very good advice on your father's part. But I don't want people to be afraid of me, especially in India."

He was thinking as he spoke that so many of the important men in the political world seemed formidable and ordinary people would find it impossible to talk to them really frankly and openly.

He always prided himself that he avoided talking down to anybody he wanted to extract information from – he tried to talk with them. But what Aisha had just said definitely raised a question.

As if she was reading his thoughts, Aisha said,

"Don't pay any attention to me. It is because you have such a strong personality that you stand out amongst other people. I expect too that a large number of women have told you that you are very good-looking."

Lord Kenington smiled,

"You are going to catch me out and accuse me of being conceited if I answer that question!"

"But, of course, you are good-looking, my Lord. In a way it is an asset you should be grateful for and cherish."

He felt he had never in his life had such a strange yet intriguing conversation with a young girl.

Aisha was talking to him as if she was either a male contemporary or, if a woman, much older than he was and at the same time he told himself she was obviously being completely frank.

It was good for him to be aware what other people thought, especially at this very moment, when he wanted to extract the truth from a large number of them.

If they were to be frightened of him, they would undoubtedly say what they thought he would want to hear, regardless of whether it was true or not.

"I suppose," Aisha said, as if she was following her own thoughts, "that we all appear different to the different people we meet."

As Lord Kenington did not reply, she went on,

"I am always surprised when people who know my Papa expect me to be as clever as he is, while other people, because I am young, are almost rudely astonished when I show any sign of being intelligent or well read."

"And you are both."

"Thank you kindly, sir!" she said mockingly. "Of course all compliments are gratefully received."

"I was not meaning to pay you a compliment, but ever since we met, Aisha, I have been astonished at some of the things you say and also at what you enjoy reading."

"I am finding the book that you lent me absolutely fascinating," Aisha remarked. "I do hope your library will last me the whole voyage."

"My library here is rather limited by lack of space. Therefore I propose that you don't gobble up my books, but read them slowly, otherwise they will not last."

Aisha laughed.

"It's impossible to read slowly when one is reading something so exciting that one feels one must reach the end to see what happens."

"I have felt like that myself, but I have learnt that if I am to absorb every word I have to do so fairly slowly. Otherwise my poor brain cannot catch up."

"I don't think we need worry about your brain, my Lord. I know you are very very clever and will take back from India exactly the information you have come to find."

"I can do so only if your father helps me and others who are working in the same field as he is."

"I have met some of them, but they would not talk to me in the same way as you and I are talking now."

"Why not?" Lord Kenington asked.

"Because Papa would not allow it," Aisha replied. "He has said to me, 'I will not have you mixed up in this.

Therefore you must not show any interest in the work of the men you meet with me and on no account are you to question them in any way that might make them think that you and I have discussed them behind their backs'."

"I think your father is very wise. As he holds his life in his hands, the least talk there is the better."

"That is the sort of thing I have been told ever since I was small," Aisha said. "But I am anxious, as you are, to know what is happening and whether those in *The Great Game* are being as successful as they want to be."

"I think it is more than likely that they are. I can only beg you to be kind and help me if you can without being indiscreet. I am sure your father would not mind our being frank with each other."

"I am not so sure about that, but, because you have been so kind to me, I must repay my debt. I promise that if I think of anything that might be of assistance to you, I will tell you about it, my Lord."

"Thank you, thank you very much indeed. And as I have already said I am greatly looking forward to meeting your father."

*

The day seemed to pass quickly.

When it began to grow dark, they went to their own cabins to read.

As she lay on her bunk, propped up against the pillows, Aisha thought just how lucky she was to have met Lord Kenington.

She now felt safe, as she would never have been able to do if she had been alone.

'He is now next door,' she thought, 'and however much Mr. Watkins wants me, he will be far too frightened of offending Lord Kenington to knock on my door.'

Before she went down to dinner, she put on one of the prettiest dresses she possessed.

She had not meant to take it out of her trunk until she reached Calcutta, but, because Lord Kenington was so distinguished, she wanted to look her best for him.

She could not help hoping that at the various ports of call on the way to Calcutta, none of his friends would come aboard.

'If he has someone else to talk to, he will not want to talk to me,' she told herself modestly.

She felt glad that at the moment there was no one of any particular interest amongst the passengers.

At dinner Lord Kenington amused her by telling her of the Cities he had visited recently and the differences he had found in the characteristics of different races.

"The Germans are aggressive," he said, "but I have to say that for amusement and charm it is impossible to beat the French."

"You are very lucky to have been to so many different Capitals in Europe," Aisha said. I have longed to explore the Far East and I would love to go to China and Japan."

"Japan is extremely beautiful and I think you would appreciate, as I did, their Monasteries and the amazing intelligence of their menfolk."

"While the Japanese women are so pretty and very feminine."

Lord Kenington smiled.

"That is true. They set themselves out to amuse and fascinate men and they do so with tremendous skill."

"Did you fall in love with a Japanese Geisha girl?"

"That is the sort of question I never reply to. I will just say that they make every effort to please a man, while an Englishwoman expects a man to please her!"

His eyes were twinkling as he spoke and she knew that he was just teasing her.

"I can see I must take lessons in Japan if I am going to be a success," she said.

"I don't think you need any lessons. Most men you meet will like you just as you are."

He thought as he spoke how very unspoilt she was and he was sure it was because that when she was at home she spent most of her time in the country.

Although she had travelled a little with her father, she had apparently either been well protected from making contact with many young men or was too pre-occupied. In fact she was completely unspoilt and everything she said and thought came naturally and spontaneously to her.

'She is certainly unique,' he reflected. 'I only hope that the Subalterns of the Army in India don't spoil her.'

When they went to their cabins after dinner, it was still quite early and Lord Kenington wanted to make notes of what he had heard from Aisha without her being aware of it.

They said goodnight outside the door.

"Thank you so much for a lovely day, my Lord, I have enjoyed every moment of it."

"Tomorrow we will be at Gibraltar," he replied, "and I will take you ashore. You will see the monkeys that everyone wants to view and the shops, which I am always told are more attractive to women than anywhere else."

"I think actually I will prefer the monkeys," Aisha replied, "but being greedy I want to see both."

Lord Kenington laughed and then he said,

"Goodnight, Aisha, sleep well and don't ruin your eyes by reading for too long."

"I will try not to and the same advice, of course, applies to you, my Lord. Goodnight and God bless you, as Mama used to say."

She entered her cabin as she spoke.

Lord Kenington remembered it was what his Nanny had always said to him when he was a small child.

He admitted to himself that he had enjoyed the day enormously and, if Aisha had not been there, he would have found no one to talk to and would doubtless have spent the day reading.

'She is very intelligent,' he told himself. 'At the same time she has told me a lot of I wanted to know about her father. It will be easy when we reach Calcutta to get him to tell me a great deal more.'

In her cabin, Aisha looked at herself in the mirror on the dressing table before she undid her gown.

Lord Kenington had not complimented her on it, but she was sure by the way he looked at her when they met before dinner that he was impressed.

He had not paid her any particular compliment and she was not certain what he thought where she herself was concerned.

'I am very very lucky to have him being so kind to me.' she thought. 'I must be careful not to bore him or to cling to him so that he thinks that I am a nuisance.'

He certainly seemed, she reflected, to have enjoyed her company today.

Their conversation had been extremely interesting and she could only think with a shiver how different the day might have been if Mr. Watkins had been pursuing her.

Slowly she took off her gown and slipped it onto its padded hanger that she had left on one of the chairs.

She crossed the cabin to where in the corner there was a curtained place for longer gowns.

Her day clothes fitted well into the cupboard which was on one side of the dressing table, but the curtained corner was, she had decided, best for her evening gowns as well as her overcoat.

Then, as Aisha pulled back the curtain to place the hanger onto the rail, she gave a scream of horror.

Hiding behind the curtain was Arthur Watkins!

He stepped out smiling and crowed,

"You thought you were free of me, pretty lady, but I don't give up so easily."

As he spoke, he seized her arm.

Then he placed one hand over her mouth so that she could not scream again.

Arthur Watkins had actually been thinking all day of how he could be in touch with what he had decided was the prettiest girl he had ever seen.

He had always moved in a Society where money was much more important than breeding or education and, because he was so rich, he was used to having any interest he showed in a woman reciprocated.

Because Aisha had avoided him, she had set him a challenge and a challenge was something that he had never refused or ignored in his busy and successful life.

In fact, because he was so successful, he had found life sometimes boring. There had not been the excitement of fighting to gain what he desired.

Usually that had been a woman and she had fallen into his arms before he had actually invited her to do so.

He did not for a single moment believe he would not overcome Aisha's fear of him and that he would be triumphant however hard she attempted to resist him.

That she had deliberately sought the company of Lord Kenington did not deceive him and because she was travelling alone and was clearly of no social consequence, he was sure that Kenington's interest in her would not last longer than the time they were at sea, if as long as that.

Arthur Watkins was not quite certain whether, as many women did, she travelled on the P & O Liner alone because it was the easiest way to find a man – one who would spend money on her and make her at the end of the voyage far better off than when it had started.

It had not struck him for a moment that Aisha was a lady by birth and thus someone who should be avoided by a man like himself.

'She's playing hard to get,' he thought, 'but it's all part of the game and I don't give up so readily.'

He had thought that Lord Kenington, being such an important individual, would soon find her a nuisance and she would then be looking round for another man.

He supposed that he had perhaps rushed his fences too quickly when he had first met her and, if she was not as experienced as most women travelling on their own were, he might have scared her.

All the same he was not completely convinced that it was not a clever move on her part.

However, as the day passed he found himself rather bored.

He looked round at the rest of the passengers, but he could see no one of any interest to him. There were a few younger women, but they were all with their husbands and children and the rest in First Class were middle-aged.

They were accompanying their husbands, who were doubtless in trade, back to India for another year or more to pass before they could go home again.

Arthur Watkins decided that he was not prepared to wait around until Kenington was bored. He would make it clear to Aisha that he would be far more generous in what he gave her than any Statesman would be.

The difficulty, he thought at dinner, was that for the moment Aisha and Lord Kenington were talking away to each other animatedly and it would be impossible for him to interrupt them.

Then, as he left the Saloon before they did, he had an idea.

He had found out earlier in the day that Aisha had changed her cabin and moved to the other side of the ship and he knew those cabins were expensive and he imagined that, by the end of the voyage, she would be wondering how she could pay for it.

'That's where I come in,' he told himself, but he was not prepared to wait.

He was bored and boredom was something Arthur Watkins was not accustomed to endure.

When he came out from dinner, he walked towards the side of the ship where he knew Aisha's cabin now was.

As he did so, he saw that her cabin door was open.

He stood still and a Stewardess came out and then, leaving the door ajar, she went down the passage.

Arthur Watkins guessed it was to collect a fresh bottle of water that Aisha would require during the night.

As the Stewardess disappeared, he slipped into the cabin and looked round for a hiding-place.

The curtain that covered the corner and the hooks on the wall was half open.

It took him only a moment to slip behind it and pull the curtain to so that he could not be seen.

He heard the Stewardess come back into the cabin and put something down and then, turning out the light, she left, closing the door behind her and locking it.

Arthur Watkins realised that he was locked in, but that did not perturb him.

He had learnt during the years in which he had made money to wait for exactly the right moment before forcing the issue.

'It will only be a question of time,' he thought to himself, 'before Aisha comes to bed and Lord Kenington, I am almost sure, will not be with her.'

He did not realise that Lord Kenington was next door, as he had not been interested in anyone's cabin with the exception of Aisha's.

One of the reasons he had made so much money was that he had concentrated fiercely and determinedly on one issue at a time. And he never relaxed for one second his insistence on getting what he wanted.

That evening he did not have to wait long.

When Aisha came into the cabin alone and locked the door behind her, he thought that he had been extremely enterprising.

Peeping through the curtain, he saw Aisha standing in front of the dressing table gazing at herself in the mirror.

Then slowly she took off the necklace from around her neck and next the dress that covered her slim body.

Because she was so lovely, Arthur Watkins felt his heart pounding and his breath coming quickly.

Then, as she crossed the floor, he realised what was going to happen and waited.

When Aisha pulled back the curtain and screamed, he realised that it might alert a Stewardess and so he put his hand over her mouth.

She struggled, but he was very strong and his right arm pulled her close against him.

"Now listen to me – " he started to say.

But she was struggling, even kicking at his legs, in an effort to get away from him.

She wanted desperately to scream out, but his hand was held tight over her mouth preventing her from making a sound.

She continued to struggle, although she felt every movement she made was ineffective against his strength.

*

In his own cabin, Lord Kenington thought that he had enjoyed the evening enormously.

All the fresh air and the exercise he had taken had made him feel more active than he had felt for a long time. He had, in fact, through overwork, been more tired than he had thought it possible to be.

He had to admit his mother was right when she had said it was good for him to take some rest and have plenty of sleep on the voyage.

As he took off his evening coat, he realised he had not told his valet to be waiting for him and, if he required the man, he would have to send a Stewardess for him.

On most evenings he let his valet, whose name was Newman, help him take off his clothes, so that he could press them ready for the next day.

But he thought tonight that there was no need to bother the man and actually, having enjoyed his time with Aisha, he had no wish to talk anymore.

He therefore was just about to undress further when there was a knock at the door.

A Steward then entered the cabin with the bottle of water he always had beside his bed.

"I'm sorry to be late, my Lord, but we've run out of the particular brand your Lordship wanted and it had to be fetched up from the storeroom."

"Thank you for taking so much trouble. I do prefer that water to any other."

"I agree with your Lordship, it's the best."

Then the Steward started.

"Was that a scream?" he asked.

"A scream?" Lord Kenington said. "I did not hear one."

"I'm sure I did, my Lord, and from the next cabin. I wonders if the lady who was dining with your Lordship is in any trouble."

Lord Kenington walked across the cabin.

"You have your master key. Open it for me."

The Steward did as he was told.

Taking his master key from his pocket, he went out into the passage with Lord Kenington close behind him.

As the Steward turned the key in the lock, he heard a man's voice and, pushing the Steward onto one side, he opened the door.

He saw Aisha struggling against Arthur Watkins, whose left hand over her mouth was preventing her from screaming again.

It only took two steps for him to reach Aisha.

Pushing her on one side, he struck Watkins a blow on the chin that lifted him off the ground and he fell back onto the floor.

He started to splutter in anger, but before he could say any more than a word, Lord Kenington dragged him to his feet.

He pulled him across the cabin, past the Steward, and struck him again so hard that he crashed down on the floor outside.

For a moment he was almost unconscious and then Lord Kenington turned to the gaping Steward and said,

"Take that swine away and, if I catch him in here again, I will myself throw him overboard. Make that clear to him."

Somewhat nervously the Steward replied,

"Yes, my Lord."

Lord Kenington took one look at Watkins, who was striving to sit up with blood pouring down his chin.

Then he went into Aisha's cabin and shut the door behind him.

She was standing with her hands clasped together wearing only her silk petticoat and, as Lord Kenington reached her, she said in a voice that did not sound like her own,

"You came – you saved me. I was so – terrified."

"I am sure you were, Aisha, and I promise you that it will not happen again. It's a disgrace to the ship and to the P & O Company that any man should behave in such a manner."

"But you saved me and, as I could not scream, I thought there was no chance of you – knowing what was – happening."

The words seemed to come jerkily from between her lips.

"It has been a nasty shock," Lord Kenington said. "Sit down on the bed for a moment while I bring you something to drink and then you must go to bed and forget it."

"You don't think – he will come again?"

"I am certain he will not again attempt anything so stupid tonight or any other night."

"You were – wonderful – my Lord," Aisha faltered.

"Fortunately I learnt to box at University," Lord Kenington added, "and it has stood me in very good stead tonight, as it has done on several other occasions."

As he was talking, he was pouring out some water from the bottle by her bed and now he handed it to her.

She had sat down on the small stool in front of the dressing table and, as she took the water, he realised that her hand was trembling.

"Hold it with both hands" he advised.

She did as she was told and, after she had drunk a little, the colour seemed to come back into her cheeks.

He thought, as he looked at her, how attractive she was with her bare shoulders and the silk petticoat showing every curve of her body.

"Now go to bed, Aisha. If you want me, knock on the wall and I will come to you at once. But I can promise you that you will not be interrupted by Mr. Watkins again tonight. If doubt if you will see him tomorrow either and I think, if nothing else, he probably lost a tooth or two in the last blow I gave him."

Lord Kenington spoke with an inner satisfaction, as he had been taught that particular punch to end a fight.

"I am sure I will be fine now," Aisha was saying, "and thank you again for being so very kind to me."

"I can promise you one thing," Lord Kenington said as he moved to the door, "that you can sleep peacefully. But I suggest you lock your door when I have left so that no one else can get in."

"I cannot imagine how he was able to come into my cabin before I came to bed," Aisha sighed.

"Forget him. I have disposed of him and I promise you that you are absolutely safe tonight and I will see that the same can be said every night on this voyage."

He smiled at her before he added,

"I will search your cabin myself, though I think Mr. Watkins will be laid up for a few days. That will give us time to make sure that there are no more Mr. Watkins's aboard!"

The way he spoke made it sound funny and Aisha gave him a little smile.

"I am sure I am quite safe now," she said. "And I will lock the door as you have told me to do."

"If you want me, knock on this wall."

Lord Kenington pointed to the wall that separated the two cabins.

Then he went out and closed Aisha's door.

She managed to rise to her feet and turn the key in the lock and then, because she felt weak, she lay down as she was on the bunk.

'How is it possible,' she asked herself, 'that all this is happening to me?'

Then, because her heart was still fluttering and it was difficult to speak, she prayed silently,

'Thank You, God, thank You for letting him save me.'

CHAPTER THREE

The next day they reached Gibraltar.

Aisha was thrilled, as Lord Kenington thought that she would be, with the monkeys running over the Rock and the shops were filled with fine goods from the Far East.

He insisted, although Aisha did protest, on buying her a shawl that had been embroidered by the Chinese.

"I have seen little boys not much older than four working on them," he told her.

"It seems cruel, my Lord, but I cannot say 'no' to such a wonderful present."

Lord Kenington felt that her enthusiasm was more genuine than he had received for much more expensive presents he had given in the past.

"We must not linger," he advised as they went to yet another shop, "because the Captain is anxious to reach Calcutta on time."

"Which I am sure he will do. This ship is far faster than any I have ever been on before."

"They are very proud of it, because it is the latest addition to their fleet," Lord Kenington declared, "and I believe it is very popular with passengers for India and the Far East by reducing the time the voyage takes."

He thought, as he was speaking, that they would pass through the Suez Canal and he was grateful that it was now there despite British opposition at the outset.

And he had often thought that it would have been very boring to have taken six weeks to reach India round the Cape. One must surely have run out of conversation being shut up for so long with the same people.

After they had left Gibraltar, the Mediterranean was the blue of the Madonna's robe and the endless sunshine made everything seem indescribably beautiful.

Lord Kenington was not at all surprised that Aisha wanted to stand in the front of the ship and watch the bow-waves breaking over the prow rather than play deck tennis.

However, somewhat reluctantly on her part before tea, they played a game and Lord Kenington won the first game and Aisha the second.

"I can see I will have to look to my laurels," he said. "I have always rather fancied myself at deck tennis."

"I am delighted and proud of having beaten you, my Lord, and I will certainly tell Papa about it with great satisfaction when we meet him."

"What I really want to know is what your father is doing at the moment," Lord Kenington enquired.

As he spoke, he wished he had not done so, because he saw a look of anxiety come into Aisha's eyes.

Equally he was aware that whatever the Liberal party might say in London, it was absolutely essential for Britain to know what the Russians were planning.

They were pushing forward their frontiers and Lord Kenington was told that the Czar's Empire was expanding by fifty-five square miles a day.

He found it hard to believe, but the British in India were indeed becoming more and more apprehensive, and to discover whether this Russian expansion was true was the reason the Prime Minister had sent him.

When he retired to bed last night, Lord Kenington had thought again that, considering who her father was, finding Aisha was one of the luckiest things that had ever happened to him.

He had been suspicious of the stories about *The Great Game.* Were those who supplied the Viceroy with so many alarming reports to be believed?

He thought a bit cynically that the young Subalterns were aware that here was a chance to escape the monotony of Garrison life and perhaps to attain promotion and glory.

Naturally they would make the most of what they were doing and he could understand that Mr. Disraeli did not want to be shown up as being over-hysterical about the Russians.

He had been given a list of more senior Officers, experienced in *The Great Game*, who it was thought would tell him the truth rather than make, as the Prime Minister was afraid, a melodrama out of the whole scenario.

"It will not be easy for you to find out the truth," he had said to Lord Kenington. "But you have never failed me in the past, and I cannot believe you will fail me now. The Liberals, as you well know, are determined that the whole thing is exaggerated and just a bogeyman to frighten us with. But from many other sources I cannot help feeling that the situation is very serious."

"I will do my best," Lord Kenington vowed.

The Prime Minister smiled.

"You always do, Charles, and that is exactly why I am sending you on what may prove to be a wild goose chase. But I would rather have your opinion than anyone else's."

He had not been particularly overwhelmed by the Prime Minister's complimentary remarks. He had heard them before and he knew that Disraeli always preferred to coax those who worked for him rather than order them.

He was aware that the Prime Minister was feeling somewhat embarrassed at taking him away from London at the height of the Season, as he knew that he was always in demand at all the best and most amusing parties.

He was a frequent guest at Marlborough House as well and when Lord Kenington told the Prince of Wales where he was going, he had not added the reason for his journey.

The Prince had, however, been instantly aware of it.

"Of course you are going to find out," His Royal Highness said, "how strong Russia is and if we need more troops in India."

Lord Kenington was not in the least surprised that he had correctly guessed why he was being sent.

Although his mother excluded him from anything to do with the Affairs of State, the Prince of Wales took the keenest interest in everything to do with the Empire.

The Affairs of State in their red boxes were locked against him, but he knew much more than Queen Victoria supposed.

Lord Kenington was extremely sorry for the Prince and thought that he was very badly treated.

"I hope, Your Royal Highness," he had said, "to get a chance of speaking to some of the senior men in *The Great Game.* They will be able to tell me the truth and will not be over-awed by the Russian advance."

"They have indeed advanced at an amazing speed," the Prince of Wales had commented. "At the same time, surely after expanding so far from home, they would not be able to take over India that easily."

"I feel just the same, Your Royal Highness," Lord Kenington replied. "But, as we know, a great number of people believe only what they want to believe and can then ignore danger until it is too late."

"Of course you are absolutely right," the Prince had said. "I can understand, Charles, that you are looking for the truth and no one could be better than you at finding it."

"Thank you, Sire," Lord Kenington had beamed.

There was a pause, then the Prince of Wales asked,

"I hope you will tell me when you return what you have discovered."

Lord Kenington thought it pathetic that, although he was the heir to the throne, he was not allowed to know any of the inner secrets of the British Cabinet nor would his mother allow him to play any part in her dealings with other nations.

"When I return you will be told exactly what I find, Your Royal Highness," Lord Kenington promised.

He saw by the expression on the Prince of Wales's face how concerned he genuinely was and how much such information meant to him.

Lord Kenington was aware that, if it was known he was passing information to the Prince of Wales, he would be severely reprimanded – not by the Prime Minister, who would understand, but by Her Majesty the Queen.

Lord Kenington had realised, when he first had his instructions from the Prime Minister that it would be very difficult to find out exactly what they wanted to know.

He was quite certain that those in *The Great Game* kept themselves very much to themselves and they made it their policy never to talk freely to anyone who like himself was not directly taking part in the defence of India.

Yet, by what almost seemed a miracle, he was now able to get in touch with one of the men who was on the secret list Disraeli had given him.

The Prime Minister had told him,

"I have put down the names of half-a-dozen men who we know are reliable and who have been in India for a long time. You may find others, but you can be quite sure that they will all keep from you as much inside information as possible.

"Why should they do that?" he had enquired.

"For the simple reason, Charles, that people talk, and talk too much," the Prime Minister had replied. "One fool returning from India had talked about his experiences, and, of course, the subject of *The Great Game* had come into the conversation. And because he had drunk freely at the party at which he was a guest, the man mentioned the name of one member he had been in contact with and two months later the man in question disappeared."

"You mean he was murdered?"

The Prime Minister had spread out his hands.

"No one knows what happened, he just vanished. But his murder, if that is what it was, is a warning not to confide in other people who, after they have visited India, are tempted to speak too freely of all that they have heard and what has taken place while they were there."

Lord Kenington understood what he was saying and vowed to himself that he would never endanger any man's life in such a careless way.

He had also wondered, if he was fortunate enough to discover the whereabouts of the men on the special list and make contact with them, whether they would trust him.

There must have been far too much said already and, as he had found in the Diplomatic Service, there were spies everywhere.

Sometimes those who cared so much for their own country were prepared to die for it, but there were those who merely found it an easy way of making money.

Whatever experiences he had had in the past, this he recognised would be the most interesting, intriguing and perhaps the most dangerous mission he had been given by the Prime Minister.

Having made contact by amazing good luck with Major Warde's daughter, he had no intention of involving her in his investigations.

They had therefore talked about a great number of other subjects, especially the countries Lord Kenington had visited which Aisha had only read about in books.

"Have you really been to Tibet?" she asked. "It is somewhere I would love to go."

"Their Monasteries, if one can get into them, are fascinating," Lord Kenington replied. "But the land over which we travelled was rough and uncultivated."

He paused as if he was thinking back.

"The Tibetans were not particularly friendly," he went on, "they were dirty and in many cases disagreeable."

"Nevertheless," Aisha said, "their faith gives them a special place in the world. I am sure, because you have been to their Monasteries, that you have learnt more about Heaven and Hell than anyone else."

Lord Kenington smiled.

"It's not quite as simple as that, but I admit I was amazed by their faith and by their extraordinary ability to foresee what is going to happen long before it does."

"How do they do that?" Aisha asked.

"I suppose we have all had a chance of doing the same, just as the Egyptians have their *Third Eye*, we too can get nearer to what is really fundamental than we do at present."

"Do you believe in prayer, my Lord?"

"Of course I do. At the same time our relationship with the *World beyond the World* is so often forgotten because we think only of ourselves and that prevents us from grasping the whole amazing wonder of it."

Aisha clapped her hands together.

"You are saying exactly what I have always wanted to hear, but I have had no one to talk to about it and the books I have read never explain it clearly."

"I know what you are saying, Aisha. I think really everyone has to find out for himself why he is born and where he is going."

He realised that this was a subject that had never arisen before between himself and a woman.

When he was in Tibet, he had talked to the Dalai Lama and the Lamas of the great Monasteries he visited.

While they devoted their lives to their religion, he came away feeling that it was a cause every man himself had to fight for and it could not, as he put it, be 'passed over the counter' to anyone who asked for it.

He found to his surprise that Aisha was exceedingly interested in what the Chinese call the *World beyond the World.*

She had read many books that he had read himself and quite a number he had not even heard about.

He had never known, although he had met a lot of women who were religious, a woman who was interested intellectually in the little that was known of the afterlife.

They talked and even argued with each other as the ship moved across the Mediterranean towards Italy.

"Do we stop at Rome?" Aisha asked him.

"I am afraid not, although I would have liked to show you Saint Peter's. Our next port of call is Naples and then it is full steam ahead to the Suez Canal."

"I am longing to see it again," Aisha said. "But I always feel as if one is sailing on sand and if you see a ship approaching from far away, that is exactly what it looks like because the level of water in the Canal is lower than the land it passes through."

Lord Kenington remembered that when in the past he had reached Suez he had always thought thank goodness half his journey was over and it would not be long before he reached his destination.

But it so interested him to hear what Aisha thought about her travels and he found that practically everything she said was original and different.

He learnt that she was impressed and influenced by the Greek Gods and Goddesses.

And she was eager to find out more about those living in the East, who believed so sincerely in the *Wheel of Rebirth*.

"Do you really think that when we all die we come back again in another body?" Aisha asked him.

"As nearly three quarters of the world believes it, it must I feel be a reasonable explanation of why we should strive and struggle to develop our minds. Surely it would be a waste if, when we die, there was nothing more for them than to be buried with us."

Aisha responded quickly,

"Oh, I am sure you are right, it is what I always thought myself. It seems such a sad waste and I am quite prepared to believe that someone as clever as my Papa has lived before. In fact I am sure of it."

"What about yourself?" he asked her.

"I am not certain who I was or what I did, but there are moments when I know what is going to happen next just as though I had seen it all in another life."

She spoke in a dreamy way and then she said,

"I am not making myself very clear, but I hope you understand, my Lord."

"Of course I do, Aisha, and I am sure that you must have been someone very bright in your last incarnation, perhaps even a man."

Aisha laughed.

"Now you are being really complimentary and you know as well as I do that no one would expect a woman, who we usually think of as being very silly, to be as clever as you are, even in another life!"

"I have not for a moment doubted your ability to argue with me and even quite often to be right," he replied.

"Now you are conceding quite a lot for the sake of argument, but in your heart of hearts you think you are superior to every woman you have ever met and which of course you are."

"Thank you, ma'am, that is very generous of you."

"It's the truth, you know it's the truth," Aisha said. "Men are cleverer than women, so that they can organise the world, while women remain at home and look after the children and make their husbands, when they do return, as happy and as comfortable as possible."

"There I agree with every word!" he exclaimed.

"Of course you do," Aisha said laughing, "and that is why we, as women, must always take second place in a world ruled by men."

"What would you want to be if you were not a woman?" Lord Kenington enquired.

"I am not going to answer that question for the simple reason that you want me to say I would like to be a man. Then you would add that I would make a very bad one! I think rather that you should learn to read other people's thoughts, which is something you should have done when you were in Tibet."

"I realise the monks can do it if they wish, but I never thought of trying to do it myself."

"Yet you live in a political world," Aisha argued, "and it would be most advantageous if you knew what your opponents were thinking and what they were planning."

"I would have thought it was impossible for anyone to know that," Lord Kenington replied.

"I think we can do it if we practise."

When he did not answer, she went on,

"Shut your eyes and think of something and I will try to tell you what you are thinking. Please don't make it too difficult, as I am only an amateur."

Lord Kenington thought she was talking nonsense, but it was different from anything he had ever done before.

He therefore shut his eyes and concentrated on the horse with which he was hoping to win the Grand National next year.

There was silence and then Aisha said slowly,

"You will win the race, but not next year, perhaps the year after."

Lord Kenington opened his eyes.

"What are you talking about?" he asked.

"You were thinking about your horses and racing a particular one, but I could not get his name. He will come in second or third next year in the big race and first another time."

Lord Kenington stared at her.

"Did you really know I was thinking about that?" he asked. "It's the most extraordinary thing I have ever known!"

"Books have told me that thought reading comes quite easily to those who devote their lives to prayer and worship," Aisha answered. "I have tried it with Papa and, now, when he is away for so long, I feel somehow that I can communicate with him, even though he is not always very aware of it."

"I have never heard anything so extraordinary. It's certainly something I would like to try myself."

"Well you must practise. It's really a question of close concentration and forcing every instinct in you into elucidating from the other person what is in their mind."

Lord Kenington laughed.

"I don't believe all this," he sighed. "How could I have come on a perfectly ordinary voyage to India and then found a young and beautiful woman who would teach me about the afterlife and other issues I have never known or even thought about myself?"

"It is something I have never talked about except with Papa," Aisha replied. "For the simple reason that I knew ordinary people would not understand and certainly would not be interested."

"And you thought I would be?"

"It seemed to come naturally into our conversation after we had talked about Tibet. It then struck me that it might be useful in what you are trying to find out when you reach India."

"I am hoping your father will help me with that."

"Papa is not the only person involved. You will find, if you can thought read, a great number of people know more about what you are seeking than you give them credit for."

"Now I am really frightened," Lord Kenington said. "While I will undoubtedly try to follow you myself, I will be extremely annoyed if anyone else reads my thoughts."

"Well, be very careful. Remember it's possible for many to do so, especially in the East."

When he went to bed that night, Lord Kenington thought he had never before had quite such an interesting time with a woman he was not actually making love to.

He had, because such issues had always interested him, been particularly intrigued in the way Aisha had read his thoughts and he was determined he would try to do it himself.

It would indeed be very useful in his political work, especially when he was confronted, as he was now, with a special mission from the Prime Minister.

At dinner they had talked of many different issues and Aisha had persuaded him to tell her about some of the strangest people he had met on his travels and these ranged from devil-dancers to the Geisha girls in Japan.

When they went to bed, Lord Kenington said,

"Now don't be frightened. I will be listening in case you need me. But I am quite sure, as there has been no sign of that unpleasant man anywhere today that he is licking his wounds in his own cabin."

"I am certain you are right. He was bleeding after you struck him the second time and I am sure he is badly bruised."

"There is no reason to feel sorry for him. Just lock your door and go to sleep."

Aisha hesitated for a moment and he asked,

"Are you still nervous?"

"Would you think it very stupid of me if I asked you to look in my cabin first to make quite sure that no one is hiding there?"

Lord Kenington smiled.

"Of course I will. I must say that I am glad you are feminine enough to be afraid of a mere man, when you associate with Gods and Goddesses and doubtless angels and archangels!"

Aisha laughed and retorted,

"Now you are poking fun at me and I will not tell you any more secrets of the universe. I will just gossip, as most people do, about everyone else!"

After Lord Kenington had found that no one could possibly be hidden in her cabin and had gone to his own, he thought over what she had said.

He decided that it was regrettably the truth.

Of course people gossiped about one another and they talked about what they had done or had not done and seldom gave a thought to anything more important.

He could hardly believe their conversation today when they had talked of Tibet and of the strange beliefs that in some countries were called religions, especially of the *Third Eye*, which the Pharaohs had proclaimed to the world by having it emblazoned on their headdress.

Lord Kenington thought that he had never expected to discuss such subjects with anyone except maybe a monk or a philosopher.

'She is really extraordinary,' he told himself, as he wondered if he could ever learn to read someone else's thoughts.

*

The ship stopped at Naples, but they were told by the Captain that they would not stay long.

He was anxious to make this voyage in a shorter time than any other P & O Liner had made it before and so he would only pick up any new passengers.

Those who had wanted to go ashore for sightseeing would unfortunately not be able to do so.

"Some people are very disappointed," Aisha said and Lord Kenington agreed with her.

"I had hoped to have a quick glance at Pompeii," she sighed. "I have read everything I can find about it."

"I am finding it very hard to believe you," he said jokingly. "I don't think you are old enough to have read all the books about Greece and Rome, besides those on other countries."

"Now you are stating that either I am a liar or I am boasting, my Lord, but I am a very quick reader and am lucky in that I can remember most of what I have read."

"Then you shall tell me what I don't know about the Gods and Goddesses of Greece when we continue our journey. In the meantime let's go on deck and see who is arriving and if there is anyone interesting amongst them. I don't mind betting you there will not be!"

It flashed through Aisha's mind that perhaps he was bored with her and so was hoping that one of his friends would turn up to make the next part of the journey more interesting for him.

Almost as if she had conjured them up, as they went up on deck, two people appeared who were obviously new passengers.

The woman was very smart and when she saw Lord Kenington she gave a little cry.

"Charles! I did not expect to see you here."

She moved quickly towards him and he answered,

"It's a surprise to see you, Mavis. I expected that you would be in London."

"Harry had to come to Italy and, as I was bored with the Season, I came with him. Now we are going on to India and I shall miss everything including seeing your horse win at Ascot."

"I will miss it myself," Lord Kenington sighed.

He shook hands with the man standing beside the lady he had been talking to and said,

"I am on my way to India too. May I introduce Miss Aisha Warde, who is also a passenger?"

As Aisha held out her hand, he finished,

"And this is the Earl and Countess of Dartwood."

The Countess gave Aisha what she thought was a quizzical look while the Earl said,

"I am not surprised to see you, Charles. You never stay in one place long enough for us to catch up with you."

"Why are you going to India in the middle of the Season?" Lord Kenington asked him.

"I had a letter from the Colonel commanding our son's Regiment, inviting us to join him in India," the Earl replied. "As I had to come to Italy to see my mother, who is living here, I thought we might as well do this part of the journey before we turned for home."

"It is lovely to see you both and I will tell you that, with the exception of Miss Warde, the company on board this Liner is very limited."

"I can well believe that," the Countess said. "That is why it is delightful for us to find you here, dear Charles. I have so much to tell you and I know you will find it all amusing."

"We had better go and see about our cabins," the Earl suggested,

Their hand luggage had been brought aboard by what was obviously the Countess's lady's maid and the Earl's valet.

They went towards the Purser's Office and Lord Kenington said to Aisha in a low voice,

"Now we are in a difficulty."

Aisha looked at him in surprise.

"Why?" she asked.

He took her arm and then drew her away from the gangway towards the bow of the ship. There was no one at their special place and instinctively they went towards it.

As they sat down, Aisha asked,

"What is wrong?"

"As you are un-chaperoned," he began, "and we are together, they will assume, whatever we tell them, that we have chosen to travel this way and it will undoubtedly be to the detriment of your reputation."

Aisha looked at him in astonishment.

Then, as he saw she did not understand, he said,

"They will think we are taking this trip just to be alone together."

The colour flooded into Aisha's face and she cried,

"Oh, I did not think of that! How very stupid of me. What shall we do?"

"I am not sure, but I do know that the Countess is a terrible gossip and so is her husband. They call him 'talkie-talkie' in White's Club. He always has far too much to say about everything and everyone!"

"I see what you mean, my Lord, but I cannot think what we can do about it, unless I get off the ship and wait for the next one."

"You must not do so as you know that I am relying on you to introduce me to your father, but you must not say so in front of the Dartwoods."

"But what can we do?" Aisha queried weakly. "It would not matter to me what they say, but, as they are your friends, you will not want them to talk about you."

"They will talk about me whatever I do or don't do. I am in fact thinking of you, Aisha."

"I am sorry, very sorry," she whispered.

"Maybe I am making a mountain out of a molehill," Lord Kenington said almost angrily. "Equally I don't want you to be talked about and I have always thought the sort of sniggering remarks that people in the Social world make about someone if they think they are having a love affair is extremely unpleasant."

He spoke in a way that told Aisha he had suffered from that sort of gossip himself.

It was indeed the truth.

Because he was so handsome and so rich and also a friend of the Prince of Wales, he had only to dance twice with the same woman for the gossip writers to say that he was having an affair with her.

When he did have one, he often felt as if it was proclaimed from the rooftops.

He was not thinking of himself at the moment, but of Aisha because she was so young and so unspoilt.

She had no knowledge of the world he lived in and that consisted of a large number of people, all very like the Earl and Countess of Dartwood.

"What we have to do," he said, "is to put our heads together and see how we can prevent these friends of mine from chattering. Unfortunately they are bound to do so, not only immediately they arrive in India, but also when they return to London."

"I don't really think it will matter much to me," Aisha said, "if that is what you are saying."

"But it will. You have not been in London, so you have no idea how the smallest thing is exaggerated, talked about and then exaggerated again until everyone believes what they last heard is the truth."

Aisha laughed.

"I have read about this sort of thing in books, my Lord, but did not believe it really happens."

"Well, it does. I would be insulting both you and your father if I did not do something to stop it."

"So what can we do?"

They sat in silence, both of them thinking fervently what they could say.

Lord Kenington was recalling that he had, when he first met the Countess nearly five years ago, thought her very attractive.

And she had flirted with him because he was so handsome. She had invited him at least a hundred times to their house in Berkeley Square and he had danced with her and kissed her in a conservatory.

But it was he, rather than she, who had decided that it should not go any further.

Lord Kenington had become very friendly with the Earl, who had invited him to shoot and also to fish on his river in Scotland.

He did not doubt, now that he was older and wiser, that if he had pursued his friendship with the Countess, it could easily have developed into an *affaire-de-coeur*.

But in those days he had been younger and shyer than he was now.

He had thought of her as a married woman and had no wish to deceive the Earl behind his back and so he had continued to be their friend over the years.

He had been aware at the same time that a number of people complained that they both talked too much.

Many of his friends in White's had moved away if the Earl sat down beside them.

'Why on earth did they of all people,' he asked himself, 'have to come aboard now?'

He was enjoying himself talking to Aisha and he had no wish to break up their friendship.

But he knew that there had already been a question mark in Mavis Dartwood's eyes when he introduced Aisha.

Aisha was now very quiet and was staring ahead.

"We have to think of something," he said. "You are clever. Now think of a way I can be looking after you and protecting you and, as far as they are concerned, have known you for many years."

"Perhaps I had better get off the ship," Aisha said. "There is just time for me to pack my clothes."

"Do you really think I would let you do that?" Lord Kenington asked. "Let them talk and be damned. I would not dream of leaving you all alone in Italy, perhaps at the mercy of men like Watkins."

He saw Aisha give a little shudder and he knew that she was frightened at the idea and he was quite certain that it would be wicked to leave anyone so pretty alone in a strange country.

"You will do nothing of the sort," he added. "We will just have to think of something sensible. There must be an answer if we can only find it."

Even as he spoke, he realised that the gangway was being pulled up and the engines were turning over.

They were pulling out of port.

Now, however difficult it might be, there was a long voyage ahead before they would reach Calcutta.

"Perhaps," Aisha suggested in a very small voice, "I could go and sit at another table for meals. Not the Captain's, because Mr. Watkins is there, but perhaps there is a nice woman somewhere amongst the passengers who would be kind to me."

There was silence and then Lord Kenington said,

"I have no wish for you to do that. I want to go on talking to you on the trip. Besides, as I have already told you the Countess is nosey and she will doubtless very soon learn that we have been together all the time up to now."

Then suddenly Aisha gave a cry.

"I have thought of something, although you may not think it good enough."

"Tell me."

"Well, do you have a cousin or a relative who is about the same age as myself?"

Lord Kenington stared at her.

"What are you trying to say," he asked.

"Tell me first," Aisha persisted.

"Yes, I have," he replied. "I do have a number of relations and I can think of at least a dozen cousins."

"Then suppose I was engaged to one of them and you were kindly taking me out to join him."

Again Lord Kenington stared at her.

"You are indeed the cleverest girl I have ever met. Of course it would be perfectly acceptable for me to be escorting you to my cousin and we could say a relative of yours, who was coming out with us, was taken ill at the last moment."

"Surely they could not object to that."

Lord Kenington was thinking.

"I have one cousin, a rather tiresome young man, who is at the moment in the Navy on one of Her Majesty's Battleships. I think he is somewhere in Africa, but it is not improbable for him to be meeting you in India, especially when I understand we have quite a number of Battleships moving in that direction as a warning to the Russians."

Aisha gave a sigh.

"Well surely, if I was engaged to him, you would be kind enough to escort me out to meet him, especially as my father is already in India and could not, at the moment, come to England to fetch me."

Lord Kenington lent back as if in relief.

"The trouble with you is that you are too bright. I am beginning to feel more and more inferior and, by the time we reach India, I may have disappeared altogether!"

Aisha laughed.

"You must remember you are chaperoning me, my Lord. It would be a great mistake to leave me until you hand me over safely to my fiancé!"

CHAPTER FOUR

Having discussed it all with Aisha, Lord Kenington went down to dinner early to find his friends.

"We must all sit together," he suggested, "as I feel sure that you don't want to sit at the Captain's table."

"Certainly not," the Countess replied. "Of course we want to be with you, Charles."

Lord Kenington lowered his voice.

"I have a secret to tell you," he said, "and I am sure you will keep it until we arrive in India."

"What is it?" the Countess asked with interest.

"I have with me and you have just met her, a very pretty girl who actually is engaged to my cousin Jack."

"Engaged!" the Countess exclaimed.

"It's being kept a complete secret until they can be together and actually she has not even told her father who she is meeting in Calcutta."

"Oh, I do understand now," the Countess said in a different tone of voice. "I wondered why such a pretty young girl was with you, Charles."

"I promised to take her out to India and we were to have a relative of hers with us, but she was taken ill at the last moment. I really don't want you to say anything or to congratulate her until her father learns of the engagement when he meets us at Calcutta."

"Of course we will keep it a secret," the Earl said. "I think Jack has done very well and he could not have a prettier wife. Where is he, by the way?"

"When I last heard from him, his ship was making its way slowly from Africa to India and he expects to be in Calcutta when we arrive or just after. When, of course, the balloon will go up," Lord Kenington said with satisfaction.

They laughed, but he knew that the Countess would not now suspect him of travelling in a most unconventional way, which she would doubtless have done otherwise.

When Aisha joined them, they were very charming to her, but made no reference to her being engaged.

Only when the men went for a walk on deck after dinner and Aisha was alone with the Countess did she ask,

"Have you known Lord Kenington for long?"

Aisha shook her head.

"No, but my family knows his family."

"Oh, I understand. So this is the first time you have been alone with Lord Kenington."

Aisha thought it was a good policy to agree to this and she nodded her head.

"Tell me what you make of him."

"I think he is very clever and most interesting."

"That is what I have always thought as well and, of course, very handsome," the Countess added.

She looked at her in a sideways manner as she said the last word and then Aisha parried,

"So are all the family. My father has often said that they are the best-looking family he has ever known."

She was making this up, but she knew the Countess was impressed.

Then they talked about clothes and the Countess had a great deal to say about the French couturiers being so much better than the English.

When the men joined them, Lord Kenington said,

"I have no intention of staying up late and actually I have a great deal of work to do while I am on board. So you must forgive me if I retire early."

"And I must do so too," Aisha added, "not because I have work to do, but because I want to finish the books I am reading on India."

"That is very wise of you," the Countess said. "I always read about the place I am going to visit so that I can be intelligent with the locals when I arrive."

"I hope not to make too many mistakes in India."

"You are not thinking of living in India, are you?" the Earl asked Aisha.

"No, of course not. I want to live in England, which I love and have good horses to ride."

This started a conversation on Lord Kenington's horses and Aisha realised she must keep out of it in case she made a wrong remark.

They then retired having said goodnight.

The Earl and the Countess fortunately had cabins on the other side of the ship.

"I think you came through that ordeal with flying colours," Lord Kenington confided to Aisha.

"I do hope so. The Countess was inquisitive about when we had met, but I said that my family knew yours and she was satisfied with that."

Lord Kenington laughed.

"I assure you she is one of the most gossipy women in England, but I believe that we have prevented her from thinking what she was longing to think about you and me."

"Why should she want to make trouble?"

"I just don't think that such women really intend to make trouble, but they like to be know-alls and would always suspect other women of doing more outrageous things than they would venture to do themselves."

Aisha grinned.

"I don't believe a word of that. I suggest that if, after I leave you in Calcutta, you meet them perhaps later on in the year, you should say that after all my engagement to Jack is broken off."

"I hope I don't have to lie unnecessarily. I have had to protect you from Watkins and now from the Dartwoods. I wonder what the third crisis will be."

Aisha gave a cry.

"Oh, don't think anything quite so horrible! I was so terrified when you first saved me and rather frightened tonight that I would make a mistake. I think if we pray fervently that we will be safe, and that is the right word for it, for as long as we are in India."

"Of course we will," he agreed. "But you must still remember that I am looking forward to meeting your father and I would only hope that he does not involve me in one of his adventurous but frightening missions."

"I will not allow Papa to do anything frightening when I am there," Aisha replied. "I only hope he will soon retire and come back to England."

"A great number of people would protest about that," Lord Kenington said. "The Prime Minister spoke of him in glowing terms and I gather he is so valuable at the moment that you will have the whole British Army against you if you try to take him away."

Aisha laughed and they had been standing outside their cabins as they talked.

"I expect you are wanting, my Lord, to get to work or enjoy yourself with one of those delightful books you brought with you. So I must not delay you any further or, of course, damage your reputation!"

"I thought it was *your* reputation we were worrying about, Aisha,"

"I am of no real importance. It is quite obvious it is you they will talk about, not me."

Lord Kenington did not argue. He merely smiled at her before he said,

"Goodnight, Aisha, and tomorrow I suggest that we start the morning with a game of tennis. I intend to beat you hollow."

"I suppose you can try, but as luck is with me at the moment or rather it is you have made me lucky, I may easily win."

"I promise you it will not be easy," Lord Kenington said, as he opened his cabin door.

His valet had left everything ready for him and, having undressed, he sat in a comfortable chair and picked up the book he was reading.

But he found himself thinking about Aisha and how clever she was and how amusing their talks had been.

Tonight at dinner he felt that he had heard from the Dartwoods the same old stories about the same people over and over again – every one of them had been either cynical or damaging to the people concerned.

And it made him wonder why gossip, especially by women, was seldom pleasant or complimentary.

The gossips made it seem as if the Social world was concentrated entirely round themselves and seldom looked further than the end of their noses.

In the next cabin Aisha thought the arrival of Lord Kenington's friends had not been as depressing as she had feared it would be.

At the same time she deeply regretted they were not still together, when they could talk on subjects that really interested her rather than just about other people.

'The people I admire,' she thought to herself, 'have either been dead for years or are explorers and adventurers. One knows so little about them and I long to know more.'

She thought that there was a question here that she might ask Lord Kenington the next time they were alone.

The difficulty was when this would happen.

*

It was in fact very difficult for them to talk together during the rest of the voyage as they steamed towards the Suez Canal and then down the Red Sea and across to India.

At night Aisha would think out questions that she longed to ask Lord Kenington and to which she was quite certain he would give her an answer.

But unless they were actually playing deck tennis, the Countess always seemed to be hovering around them, monopolising Lord Kenington and making it clear that he must talk to her.

And the result was that Aisha had to keep silent or disappear.

It was only their tennis and that Lord Kenington insisted on walking round the deck in the morning, when Aisha could accompany him, that made it possible for them ever to be alone together.

The Earl and Countess sat with them at every meal and, whenever they found a quiet secluded place on deck, the Countess invariably appeared after they had been there only a few minutes.

It was when they were within sight of Calcutta that Aisha said a little wistfully to Lord Kenington,

"I do hope we will meet again. There are so many questions I want to ask you, but since Naples I have never had the chance."

"And I should have enjoyed answering them," Lord Kenington replied. "But of course we will meet again. When I meet your father, I will ask him if he will come and see me tomorrow and, of course, you must come too."

Aisha smiled.

"I would enjoy that. But it will not be the same as being able to talk as we did on the first part of the journey on every possible subject."

"We certainly covered the world," he laughed, "but I think there is still a great deal more for us to find out or is it perhaps hidden away in Heaven?"

"Then we must still find it and dissect it between us!" Aisha replied.

"I will tell you what we will do – " he said.

At that moment an all too familiar voice piped up,

"Oh, here you are, Charles. I wondered where you could be. I have been looking for you everywhere."

"We were just saying that, with Calcutta in sight, it will not be long now before we will all be saying goodbye to each other," Lord Kenington replied.

"I hope that's not true," the Countess said. "You will be going on to Simla to see the Viceroy and so will we after we have visited the Colonel."

"Oh, that is splendid news."

There was nothing else he could say.

*

It was afternoon and the sun was very hot when the Liner sailed into Port at Calcutta.

Aisha had already been on deck for half-an-hour, waiting eagerly for the first sight of her father.

When Lord Kenington joined her, he said,

"You must not forget that I am almost as eager to see your father as you are."

"But for very different reasons, my Lord. I am sure that he will be here waiting for me and he will tell you where we are staying."

"I expect it will be at Government House, unless your father is at Regimental Headquarters."

"We will soon find out the answer."

She was looking very pretty, wearing a thin cotton dress because it was so hot. Also a shady hat trimmed with flowers.

Lord Kenington suddenly thought that if she was to meet the Officers of her father's Regiment, as undoubtedly she would, he would have even less chance of being alone with her as they had been onboard.

They waited for the ship to come slowly alongside.

Lord Kenington was immediately aware that Aisha suddenly stepped nearer to him.

He could see that Arthur Watkins was only a little way from her.

When he saw Aisha share a table with the Earl and Countess of Dartwood, Watkins had been astute enough to realise that he had made a mistake about her.

He knew enough of the Social world to be aware that, if she was the type of woman he had thought her to be, the Earl and Countess would not for one moment have sat down at the same table beside her.

In other words she was a lady and, although she was travelling alone, she was not what he had assumed. Nor would she behave in anything but a ladylike way.

'I have made a fool of myself,' Arthur Watkins told himself, as he deliberately walked away from Aisha.

She gave a sigh of relief.

"Forget him," Lord Kenington said. "It's something that happens to pretty girls all over the world and you should never think about it again."

"Now you are reading my thoughts, as I told you to do. Incidentally it's an experience I will not forget easily."

"Of course you will. When you are engrossed with India and only India, and perhaps with the charming young gentlemen who will be praising you to the skies from the moment you appear."

"I only hope that's true, but I think it's unlikely. Now at last we ought to see Papa."

She leant over the railing as she was speaking and Lord Kenington stood beside her.

He wondered what her father would look like. He expected him perhaps to be in uniform, which would make it easier to identify him.

Although there was a throng of people waiting on the quay, Aisha did not point anyone out.

In fact, when at last they went down the gangway, there was a carriage waiting for the Earl and Countess, which had been ordered in advance, but there was still no sign of Major Warde.

"I cannot think where he can be," Aisha sighed.

"Of course you let him know that you were sailing on this ship?" Lord Kenington enquired.

"Of course I did and I received a reply from him, saying that he would meet me on arrival. But here I am and there is no sign of him."

They stood to one side so as not to be pushed about by the crowd disembarking from the lower decks.

There were a large number of Indians among them and the colourful saris of the women looked very pretty in the sunshine.

Finally, when it seemed as if the ship must be now completely empty, Lord Kenington proposed,

"Well, as your father has not turned up, I suggest that you come with me to Government House, where I am going anyway and we will find out if they have any news of him."

He knew by the expression in Aisha's eyes that she was worried that he might be in danger.

Then he said quickly,

"Don't get upset. He may have been held up in a dozen different ways and you should know that the time of day in India varies from person to person, in fact an Indian is invariably too late or too early."

"That does not sound at all like my father – "

Their luggage, however, was piled onto a carriage and Lord Kenington, who had not asked to be met, told the coachman to drive directly to Government House.

When they arrived and Lord Kenington said who he was, they were taken at once to the Officer in command of the troops in Calcutta who was a General.

He greeted Lord Kenington with delight.

"We knew that you were coming out, my Lord," he said. "But unfortunately I was not told which ship you would be on."

"Actually I was not certain myself until the very last moment, but I knew it would be easier to come here first to you and find out how soon I can see the Viceroy."

"That means going up to Simla, as you probably expected, my Lord," the General declared.

"Well, at least I am here and now may I introduce Miss Aisha Warde, who was expecting her father, Major Warde, to be meeting her on the quay."

The General stiffened.

"Is Major Warde your father?" he asked Aisha.

"He is and he promised to meet me here. I had a telegram from him saying that he would be on the quay at Calcutta as soon as the P & O Liner reached Port."

They were in the General's private room and there were two desks and a man was seated at one of them.

The General walked across and spoke to him in a low voice so that Aisha did not hear what was said.

The man immediately went from the room, closing the door behind him and the General indicated a sofa and comfortable armchairs on one side of the room.

"I have ordered you something cool to drink," he said, "which you will certainly need in this climate. I have also asked my assistant to find out the latest news of Major Warde."

Aisha gave a cry.

"You mean he is out on a mission?" she asked.

"I really don't know what he is doing," the General replied. "But they expected him back at the Regiment several days ago."

Aisha did not speak, but Lord Kenington knew just what she was feeling.

He put out his hand and took hers.

"It may be only a slow train or a lazy mule that has delayed your father," he said. "So don't panic before we know exactly what has happened."

"I will try not to," she answered nervously.

Her fingers trembled in his and he did not release her hand.

A servant brought the cool drinks and, while they were sipping them, the General left the room.

"What can have happened to Papa?" Aisha asked when they were alone.

"Now you must not get upset," Lord Kenington replied. "You know as well as I do that things are very different in India. There are a hundred ways he could be delayed and not one of them what you might expect."

"Of course I expect it to be something frightening. You know, as well as I do, that Papa takes risks that no ordinary man does."

"As he is brave, you have to be brave too. I am quite certain that it is nothing really concerning."

Even as he spoke he knew that any man who played *The Great Game* held his life in his hands.

At the same time Major Warde had a tremendous reputation and was very experienced. He would obviously not take unnecessary risks, especially at a time when he was expecting to welcome his daughter.

The General came back into the room

"I am afraid I have no news," he said, "either good or bad. Your father, Miss Warde, went off on a special mission three weeks ago and we have been expecting to hear from him ever since. It was not a very difficult one and they are confident that he will turn up at any moment."

"Thank you for finding that out," Aisha said. "But what am I to do in the meantime?"

"One suggestion," the General replied, "is that you go straight to Simla, because that is where your father will go if he has the information we expect from him."

"You mean he will need to report to the Viceroy?" Lord Kenington asked.

The General nodded.

"The Viceroy and, as it so happens, one of our Staff Officers, who knows more about this mission than anyone else does, is actually with the Viceroy at this moment."

"Then that is where we are going," Lord Kenington replied. "It will be very easy for me to take Miss Warde with me."

"I thought you would say that, my Lord, it certainly saves my having to find someone to chaperone and look after her, which of course she must have."

He thought for a moment and then he added,

"I think it would be best for you and Miss Warde to stay here until nine o'clock this evening when you can then take the night train to Simla. That train is certainly the most comfortable way of going there."

"I agree with you," Lord Kenington replied, who had been on the night-train before. "Of course we will be very grateful for your hospitality until we leave."

"Luncheon will be ready in about half-an-hour," the General said. "In the meantime any luggage you require can be taken up to a bedroom so you can rest afterwards. Or, of course, if you prefer, go sightseeing."

"I think we would be happy to stay in the garden if it is not too hot," Lord Kenington answered. "I would also like a swim."

"The swimming pool is there waiting for you," the General smiled. "I hope Miss Warde will ask for anything she requires from my housekeeper, who I may say is a very reliable woman who has looked after us all for years."

Aisha was pleased to find a comfortable bedroom that looked out over the garden.

When she went down to luncheon, it was to meet a large number of soldiers most of them Majors or Colonels and there were a few distinguished Indians present.

And she was quickly surrounded by men who were, Lord Kenington noted, overcome by her beauty.

She certainly looked very lovely and he thought that she would find in India, as he had prophesied, many men who would lose their hearts to her.

Lord Kenington swam in the afternoon, but, as it was very hot, Aisha just watched him.

Then they had a short rest after tea before an early dinner at Government House and leaving for the station.

The station at Calcutta had always seemed to Lord Kenington to be one of the most extraordinary sights in the world.

It amused him, as it amused Aisha, to see people sleeping on the platform as they waited for a train going the following day. Many of them were accompanied not only by their children but by their animals.

There was a continual roar of trains coming in and going out and bands that apparently had nowhere else to practise were also on the station.

British travellers, who seemed rather out of place, shouted at their bearers if they did not get exactly what they wanted the moment they asked for it.

Even to look round was to see life in a completely different aspect from how it was in England.

Lord Kenington watched Aisha taking it all in and then he said,

"I knew this would delight you. The first time I came here it looked like a pantomime I had seen as a child, but more spectacular than anything staged at *Drury Lane*."

"Everything seems to be happening at once," Aisha remarked. "But you can understand why to the Indians it is a real adventure to travel by train."

"Let's hope it will be an adventure for us as well," Lord Kenington commented.

Because he was such an important visitor, they had a private drawing room attached to the train to take them to Simla.

It consisted of two bedrooms, a drawing room with comfortable chairs and a small pantry that contained all the drinks and food they would require on their journey.

Aisha explored it with delight.

"It's like a doll's house," she enthused. "Papa told me a little about the trains in India, but he did not mention this to me."

"This is because we are deemed so important and I am delighted. But I doubt I would have been given one, if you had not been with me."

"You cannot expect me to believe that even though they are obviously impressed by Papa."

"Shall we say it is a combination of your father and the Prime Minister?" Lord Kenington mused. "At least we can be comfortable and have some time alone."

"Now I can ask you all my questions," Aisha said. "Perhaps I will have to keep you awake all night!"

"I warn you that after a good dinner and, I hope, some excellent wine, I will just agree to everything you say," Lord Kenington replied teasingly.

"That would be most unkind of you. Does that mean you will not answer my questions after I have been so patient and did not bother you after the Dartwoods came aboard?"

"It is something you were unable to do anyway and I am thankful that we have left that chatterbox behind us, although regrettably she will be joining us in two or three days at Viceregal Lodge."

"I will have left by that time with Papa. He has promised me that he will show me India and I have made a list of the places I want to see. So we will not be staying with the Viceroy, I hope, for more than a night or two."

"I have a feeling you are being very selfish. I want to talk to your father and I want to talk to you and I very much doubt if I can do it in two days."

"You might have to try, my Lord."

He threw up his hands as if in despair.

Before the train, after a great deal of puffing and blowing, steamed off, a Steward came to see what was in the pantry and to bring them any drink they fancied.

As they had already dined in Government House, neither of them was hungry, but they gladly accepted long iced drinks.

Finally, when the train, making much ado about it, moved out of the station, Aisha felt a feeling of joy.

Now at last she was on her way to her father and she felt that it was reasonable to believe that he would be at Simla.

His mission was in that direction, but the only issue that seemed a little disturbing was that he had not arranged for anyone from Government House to meet her.

That meant he had been quite certain he would be there himself and would have time to come to Calcutta after having seen the Viceroy.

'I am sure he will be there,' she told herself again reassuringly.

As once more Lord Kenington was reading Aisha's thoughts, he said,

"Of course he will be. Stop worrying and enjoy India. Let's count our blessings that we are doing it so comfortably."

"I will try to do so, my Lord, and now let's talk of other things. I want you to tell me, as you promised to do, but we did not have the time, about the special Monasteries you visited in Nepal."

Lord Kenington laughed.

"Have I come all this way," he asked, "entirely to improve your geography?"

"That is not geography, it is food for the mind or perhaps I should say, for the soul. After all, you have had your dinner, so I am entitled to mine."

"I might have guessed you would have a very good excuse for making me talk. I really was thinking of resting until I had to meet the Viceroy."

"Another thing you can do, which might be easier at the moment, is to tell me about him," Aisha suggested.

"I will tell you one story which will amuse you. Thirty-six years ago, in fact in 1840, when Disraeli was a young man, he visited one of the private schools and, when he was there, he gave a small boy a half sovereign. It was the first he had ever received."

"Then he must have been delighted. I suppose you are going to tell me it was the Earl of Lytton."

"It was, and Disraeli said later, 'now I have tipped him again and this time put a crown on his head'."

Aisha laughed.

"I am sure that that is something Lord Lytton will always remember."

"I think that you will find him charming," Lord Kenington said. "He has been a great success so far in this country. I will be interested to know, as you have not met him before, if you find him not only handsome but with a charm that few Englishmen possess."

"My father said the same sort of thing about him."

"Your father is not the only person and nor am I. The Queen found him delightful and said 'he is a man full of feeling'."

"I suppose that is high praise," Aisha said, as she thought it over. "It is usually left to the women to do the feeling in a family!"

Just to be argumentative Lord Kenington took the opposite view and once again they were off on one of their duelling conversations that they both found so fascinating.

It was when they made the next stop and looked out at the darkness that Lord Kenington said,

"I think now I must send you to bed. You will find that in India people wake very early. In fact they usually get up with the first rays of the sun. You will doubtless be woken long before you wish to from the delightful dreams you will undoubtedly have because you are in India."

"I dream almost every night," she admitted. "That is another subject I have to talk to you about."

"Well, we have all tomorrow, but now, as you must get your beauty sleep before Viceregal Lodge, you must go to bed as soon as the train starts again."

A Steward was already on board preparing more cooling drinks for them. There were also delicious biscuits to eat if they felt hungry during the night.

When the Steward had left and the train started off again, Aisha commented,

"This is certainly comfort in a very big way. I cannot think why our trains in England are always over-crowded and so much less comfortable."

"In England we would not have our own drawing room to ourselves. So you must thank your lucky stars for being amongst the Rulers of this country and thus being treated like a Queen."

"That is one thing I have never wanted to be."

"But why" Lord Kenington asked, "I thought it was every woman's dream."

"Of course not, a Queen is always in the public eye and people criticise almost everything she does. It must be frightening waking up every morning knowing it would be fatal not only to yourself but to many other people if you made a mistake."

"I did not think of it like that. The funny thing about you, Aisha, is that you always think of something new and unexpected to say! I think you should be paid for being a 'Master of the Mind'."

Aisha laughed.

"That will be the day, when any woman has a job like that. Even you automatically said, 'Master of the Mind' and not 'Mistress of the Mind'. You instinctively think of anyone in authority as being male and not female."

"I think I was speaking about Her Majesty, Queen Victoria."

"But she is an exception to every rule as you well know. There is not another Queen who has ever been so magnificent or has ruled over so vast a territory. Yet she is a woman, which is perhaps why we have to work even harder to keep places like India under the Union Jack."

They talked on before Lord Kenington declared,

"It is getting late and I am losing the argument. I am therefore going to bed to polish up my brain. I intend to defeat you on every subject tomorrow morning simply because I am a man!"

"Do you really think I would allow you to do that?"

"I doubt if you would be able to prevent me from dominating our conversation," Lord Kenington replied.

He knew that it would stimulate her once again into fighting him, but instead she laughed.

"It's wonderful," she sighed, "to be here alone with you and to be able to talk as we have just been. I missed it so much after Naples. And I used to go to bed and try to pretend I was you and answer my arguments with what you would have said."

"I hope I was successful," Lord Kenington grinned.

"Only occasionally. Then, of course, I had to try even harder to defeat you the next time."

"As I will try tomorrow. I still think it's amazing that, looking like you do and being so young, you can talk to me as if you were the Viceroy, the Pope and a few distinguished philosophers all rolled into one!"

Aisha gave a little cry.

"That is the nicest thing anyone has ever said to me! Thank you, thank you! I feel so happy being with you that for the moment I have stopped worrying about Papa."

"Now I am trying to read your father's thoughts that he will come back to you safely."

"I want to believe you and therefore I *will* believe you," Aisha answered.

She rose from the comfortable sofa and walked towards her bedroom.

"Goodnight, my Lord, and thank you for being such a wonderful man that I am almost prepared to admit you are always right!"

She closed her door as Lord Kenington did not answer.

He was laughing as he went into his bedroom that was opposite hers.

CHAPTER FIVE

Aisha found the whole of the next day entrancing.

There was so much varied and interesting scenery to watch from the windows of their drawing room on the train.

Above all she had the whole day in which to talk to Lord Kenington, to have his undivided attention and to discuss so many of the subjects she had in mind.

When she went to bed that night, she thanked God for giving her such a happy day, so happy that she had almost forgotten to worry about her father.

Aisha had again slept peacefully in what she found was a surprisingly comfortable bed.

Lord Kenington was obviously in a cheerful mood and the sun was shining and everything seemed wonderful.

A carriage was waiting for them at the station to drive them to Viceregal Lodge.

"I know nothing at all about the Viceroy's house in Simla," Aisha said as the horses drove off. "Tell me about it, my Lord."

"Apparently, Lord Lytton had a bad impression of it when he first saw it. He described it to his friends as 'a mere bivouac'. He found 'Peterhof', as it is nicknamed, uncomfortably small and he complained he could never be alone there."

"What did he mean by that?" Aisha asked.

"He said the sentries outside his window were too close for one thing and that 'three unpronounceable beings in white and red nightgowns' rushed after him if he walked about indoors. And, if he set foot in the garden, he was 'stealthily followed by a tail of fifteen persons'."

"I don't believe it," Aisha laughed.

"Nor do I, but it made a good story."

"But I have always heard that the people of Simla are the most amusing and, of course, there are innumerable visitors from England."

"Unfortunately, the Viceroy really prefers Paris to anywhere else and in fact he said to a friend of mine only a few weeks ago, 'I do so miss the pleasant scamps and scampesses of glorious France'!"

"Now you are telling me things I have not thought of before," Aisha said. "I heard that everyone in England and India thinks that he is one of the best Viceroys we have ever sent."

"You will find him charming, as I do. At the same time I would rather agree that he would be more at home in France than he is in India."

It did not take them long to drive from the station to Peterhof.

Aisha thought it smaller and not as attractive as she had imagined it would be, but the garden was lovely with a mass of flowers, which would have been just impossible in Calcutta at the moment owing to the heat.

When they were shown into the reception room, Lord Lytton was already there.

He held out his hands in delight when he saw Lord Kenington.

"Charles!" he exclaimed. "I have been counting the days until you arrived. There are a great number of matters I want you to help me with."

"And I have come to India especially for your help, Robert," Lord Kenington replied, "so we will have to take it in turns!"

"All that matters is that you are here," Lord Lytton said, patting him on the shoulder.

Then he looked a little curiously at Aisha.

"I have brought with me," Lord Kenington said quickly, "Miss Aisha Warde. She was due to be met by her father, Major Harold Warde, at Calcutta, but he did not turn up. So I brought her here as she had nowhere else to go."

"But, of course, that was the only thing you could do and I am delighted to meet Miss Warde," the Viceroy said.

After glancing round the room where there were several people at the other end, he suggested in a low voice,

"I think you should come into my study."

Lord Kenington was immediately aware that this invitation was connected with Aisha's father.

"That would be a good idea," he said, "and I have some important news for you from the Prime Minister."

"Come along," Lord Lytton invited them.

He went ahead and Aisha thought he was certainly very good-looking, although she did not really admire a man with a beard.

But she could understand, from the way he moved and the way he talked, why he had often been described as looking like a nervous thoroughbred.

It was not that he was horse-faced. In fact he was one of the most handsome men she had ever seen. He had a lofty brow and a prominent finely shaped nose.

She was to learn later, when she knew him better, that his likeness to a racehorse was not in his physical features, but in his temperament and it showed in his face and his expression as well as in his air of breeding and distinction.

His study was a very attractive room overlooking the garden.

Having shut the door, the Viceroy turned to Aisha,

"I am afraid that I have upsetting news about your father and you are naturally worried that he did not meet you at Calcutta."

Instinctively Aisha put out her hand towards Lord Kenington, who took it in both of his.

"What has happened," she asked in a scared voice.

"Nothing so far that is very desperate," Lord Lytton replied, "but he has not turned up at Headquarters as he was expected to do nearly a week ago and we are rather afraid that he has run into trouble."

"You mean the Russians have taken him prisoner?" Aisha asked.

"Not as bad as that, I hope," the Viceroy replied. "But he might have lost his way or perhaps been unable to get to where he could travel to where he wants to go, which naturally is here."

Aisha looked up at Lord Kenington.

"What can we do?" she asked anxiously.

"I am afraid nothing until we know more," Lord Kenington said quietly.

He helped her to a sofa, then sat down beside her.

He turned to Lord Lytton, who had seated himself at his desk,

"Now please do tell us a little more, Robert. You realise what a shock this is to Aisha, after coming out at her father's request and expecting him to be meeting her."

"I can understand what she is feeling and I think she is being very brave," Lord Lytton replied. "At the same time I admit we are worried about Major Warde."

"Where did he go and was he in disguise?" Lord Kenington enquired.

"Of course he was. No one could disguise himself more effectively than Harold Warde."

"I suppose you know where he went and what he was trying to find out?"

"I understand that he went at his own suggestion, because he had some idea of what he might find. But he did not impart the information to anyone and told no one exactly where he was going."

"No one?" Lord Kenington said questioningly.

"He merely said he had reason to believe that there was trouble in a part of the country only a short distance from here and that he would investigate it and bring me a report before he left for Calcutta to meet his daughter."

There was silence and then Lord Kenington said,

"Can you send people to look for him?"

"They are already out looking to the best of their ability, but, as Warde did not give them full particulars of what he was attempting to discover, they have so far not been successful.

"I am sure Miss Warde will be very brave, as one expects from her father's daughter and will try to behave amongst my guests as if nothing is wrong. It would be a great mistake for any of them, however charming they may be, to suspect that we are facing any kind of trouble."

"Yes, of course, I understand that," Lord Kenington replied. "And I am sure that Aisha does too."

"I can only pray that Papa will be found as soon as possible," Aisha added a little shyly.

She spoke very quietly and Lord Kenington thought that no one could behave with more self-control.

He was used to women when anything went wrong, crying and sobbing and making a to-do about everything and then the nearest man felt obliged to comfort them.

Aisha had released Lord Kenington's hand and was now sitting with her hands in her lap and only because he now knew her so well was he aware she was trembling.

"What I want you to do," the Viceroy said, "is to enjoy yourself if it is at all possible and, if not, pretend you are having a good time."

"I will – try," Aisha stammered.

He smiled at her.

"I thought you would. It is essential, when things happen like this, that the trouble, whatever it may be, is not discussed by people who don't understand what they are saying, especially in front of the servants."

He paused before he added,

"I am sure, as your father's daughter, you are aware of that danger."

"Of course I am and I promise you, my Lord, I will be very careful. I just want my father returned to me as soon as possible."

"It is what we are all hoping," Lord Lytton said. "As you well know, your father is greatly admired for the splendid work he has done here. I will let you into a secret when I tell you he is on the Honours List for next year, when he tells me he is retiring. I am sure, when he returns to England, he will make his name in the House of Lords."

"I am, of course," Aisha said quietly, "delighted to hear that all he has done for England has been appreciated. But I hope now that you will make every effort to find him, my Lord."

"I promise you we are doing so. There is always a chance in this part of the world that he may have slipped and hurt himself so that he is unable to walk or he may have gone further away from here than he intended and is taking longer to come back than he expected."

Aisha realised that he was only trying to cheer her up by being as encouraging as possible.

When she saw the look that the Viceroy gave Lord Kenington, she realised that both men were worried.

"I would like now," Lord Kenington said, "if your Lordship will permit, to take Miss Warde round the garden to admire the flowers. Having been shut up in that train all night, we need the air. Then later, if you agree, I would like to see you alone."

"Yes, of course, Charles, and I think you are quite right to take Miss Warde into the garden. It will be hotter after luncheon, when I am certain you will need a siesta."

"You are very kind and understanding, Robert."

Lord Kenington rose to his feet as he was speaking and Aisha rose to hers.

They walked out through a side door and onto the lawns.

They could feel a faint wind coming from the hills and they were certainly very beautiful in the distance.

They walked in silence until they found a wooden seat in front of a pool. It was sheltered overhead by the boughs and leaves of an olive tree.

"Let's sit down," Lord Kenington suggested.

"If you are going to tell me not to worry, I shall scream," Aisha said. "I am desperately worried about my Papa and it's no use pretending that I am not."

"Of course you are," he agreed, "and so am I. But a hundred things can occur unexpectedly in India and one of them could easily be the reason why he is not here yet."

"I felt sure that something was wrong when we reached Calcutta."

"So did I, but you have been very brave, Aisha, and as your father's daughter you cannot display your emotions publicly."

"I have no intention of doing so, my Lord, because I know that might be dangerous too. I just wish that there was some way we could get in touch with him."

There was silence for a moment and then she said,

"You were telling me last night how the monks could communicate with each other over long distances. How do you think they managed it?"

Again there was silence and then he answered,

"I think in some way it is the same as when you try to read my thoughts and I try to read yours. The monks, of course, prayed and their prayer reached the man for whom they were praying. In some strange way he responded."

"You mean they could trace him even if he was miles away?" Aisha asked.

"Exactly. Perhaps one day in the future we will have an instrument with which we can talk to people who are a long distance from us. But now the only people who have managed to do it have been the monks of Tibet."

"Why did you not ask them to teach you?"

"I tried to find out everything I could from them, but something like that was beyond anyone who had been brought up to believe just what he could see with his eyes."

Aisha sighed.

"If only we could be in touch with Papa now. I was thinking, as I walked through the garden, that I would send out my thoughts to him. If he sent his back to me, then perhaps I would know where he was."

"We can only try, but you must not be disappointed if you fail, Aisha. After all, there are many secrets in the East, which we have not even heard about in the West."

"I will try to get in touch with Papa and, please, it would help me if you tried too, my Lord."

"Of course I will, but I am afraid I am a very practical person and I find it difficult to believe that these things happen, even though it has been actually proved to me that they do."

"It does seem wrong, when we fancy ourselves as an advanced nation, with our education better than most, that we don't try to emulate some of the amazing results of thought that are achieved by people in this country and in other countries in the East."

"I know exactly what you are saying," he replied, "but, as I have said, we are not an imaginative people and we like everything that is set in front of us to be positive. Also intelligible, so that we can add it up and find that two and two make four."

"But the monks have told you their brains can fly into the sky and reach each other hundreds of miles away, while we can painstakingly only build a railway or a road if we want to reach some distant place."

"That is called being civilised," Lord Kenington said with a smile.

"I think you are laughing at me, my Lord, but Papa would understand."

"And I assure you I understand too, but I am trying to make you practical and let me say you are behaving wonderfully well and very sensibly."

"I am trying to, I am really trying very hard," Aisha replied. "But I want to scream and run and find Papa for myself. I am sure if I tried, I could find him!"

He was sure that she did not really mean it.

He merely put his hand over hers and said,

"We must both be very careful not to let anyone else know that we are worried. On occasions like this it is always wise to think of the person you are looking for. You are acting a part, but not for one moment must you let people be aware that you are acting. That is why you have to concentrate and be exceptionally intelligent."

"I will try, I really will try," Aisha promised. "But you must admit, my Lord, that, having come all this way, it is terrifying that Papa was not waiting for me."

"Of course it was, but he would be the first person to tell you not to endanger him or anyone he is with by letting anyone else know that you are actually perturbed."

"I will pretend that I am enjoying this lovely place and find everyone in it very agreeable," Aisha said. "But you will have to help me and it's not going to be easy if, as the hours go by, there is still no sign of Papa."

"Of course I will help you, Aisha, and, as I now see people approaching in the distance, we might go into the wood and enjoy the shade of the trees."

She jumped up at once and they moved away from the people coming towards them.

Despite the Viceroy saying that Peterhof was too small, there were always people staying there and, as Lord Kenington well knew, there would be a large number of guests for luncheon and for dinner every day.

When they had luncheon, Aisha found that she was seated between two good-looking young men who had come to Simla to play polo.

They were both experienced players and were very determined that their team should beat everyone they were playing against.

They talked of their sport and at the same time they paid Aisha endless compliments, which she found amusing rather than embarrassing.

Watching her from the other side of the table, Lord Kenington thought that she was putting on a very good act.

In fact she appeared completely carefree and out for enjoyment and she was also looking extremely attractive.

He was well aware that, because they had arrived together, the other women staying in Peterhof were already linking them and this irritated him

He had, with great dexterity, avoided being married for many years now and he had no intention of rushing up the aisle.

He was accompanying a young girl he was very delighted to be with simply because of her father.

When he had said goodbye to the Earl and Countess of Dartwood, they had asked him somewhat pointedly, he thought, when the marriage between Aisha and his cousin would take place.

"I have not the slightest idea," he had responded, "when Jack will get leave or if his ship is required on duty in some obscure part of the globe where wives are not particularly welcome."

He deliberately made the whole scenario sound as vague as possible and as if he himself was not particularly interested.

Equally he was not at all sure if the Countess was deceived and he knew that if it was reported that he was travelling alone with a young girl who was as beautiful as Aisha, the whole of London would be discussing it.

In which case there would be no escape.

He had not told the same story when he arrived in India for the simple reason that there was no need for it.

He had met Aisha travelling on the ship, he said, and immediately became aware that she was the daughter of Major Warde and he would have been very stupid if he had not made himself pleasant to her.

If no one else understood the reason, the Viceroy would.

He made a mental note to make sure if possible that no one in Simla became aware that Aisha had come from England alone and un-chaperoned, as he knew the mere fact that they had arrived together to stay with Lord Lytton would be enough to set the tongues wagging.

And especially if they knew that they had shared a private drawing room on the train and that no other woman had been present.

To stop these tongues Lord Kenington decided that now he should concentrate on flattering and flirting with the pretty women staying in the house.

He realised that he must pay as little attention to Aisha as possible, although they shared the secret of her father's disappearance.

He knew that she was relying on him to help her and to keep her from being more distressed than she was already.

Therefore he had to be there if she wanted him and he felt that it was his duty to support her in every way he could.

*

The day passed slowly.

Shortly after tea Lord Kenington went alone to the Viceroy's private room and found him working at his desk.

As he closed the door behind him, he asked,

"Is there any news? I know it's a silly question as you would have sent for me if there had been."

"Of course I would," the Viceroy replied. "Do sit down, Charles, and tell me about this lovely girl you have brought with you. I had no idea that Harold Warde had a daughter. She is certainly one of the most beautiful women I have seen for a long time."

"I felt exactly the same when I first saw her," Lord Kenington replied. "And she has the most amazing brain, which naturally she must have inherited from her father."

"You can be sure of that," the Viceroy agreed. "I can tell you in all sincerity that Harold Warde is one of the most brilliant men I have ever met.

"If we lost him it would be an absolute disaster. I cannot tell you how magnificent he has been these last few months and what priceless information he has managed to obtain for us."

"That is exactly what I want to talk to you about, Robert, and why the Prime Minister has sent me to you."

"I am aware of your mission, but Prime Minister or no Prime Minister, I am delighted to see you, Charles. I am sure that you can help us with some of our problems, which seem to grow more difficult every day."

"What is happening?" Lord Kenington enquired.

"It's the Russians, always the Russians! They are coming closer and closer to us and I want you to get it put firmly to the Cabinet in England that we must have their support and more troops."

"Is that really necessary, Robert?"

Lord Lytton nodded.

"I am not saying they will all be used, but a show of strength will, if we use it sensibly, prevent Russia from taking the final step of attempting to wrest India from us."

"Do you really think they will be so stupid? After all, they have to come thousands of miles to meet an Army that is well-trained and provided with up-to-date weapons."

"I think that the threat from the Russians is slightly exaggerated," Lord Lytton replied. "At the same time they are a definite menace and I would like people at home to appreciate it."

"That is exactly why I am here, Robert."

"I know, but you can be certain that Gladstone's lot will say that you have exaggerated the whole thing and that you have not delved deep enough to find the real trouble."

"They talk and they talk," Lord Kenington replied. "But I can assure you that I will be very firm about this and the Prime Minister said that he would value my advice above anyone else's."

"I agree with him," Lord Lytton smiled, "but you know how pig-headed they all are and it would take a sledge-hammer to awaken most of them to danger."

Lord Kenington grinned.

"It's not as bad as that, although people do believe what they want to believe. However, I will be on stronger ground when I can hear details from Warde. What do you really think has happened to him?"

"I don't mind telling you," Lord Lytton replied, "that I am terrified he has been captured. He is, without exception, the best man we have in the whole of *The Great Game* and at assuming disguises he is superb."

He paused for a moment before he went on,

"I defy anyone to recognise him when he is dressed as a Holy man or as a mere Sudra. His own mother would be deceived when he is playing such a part."

"You have men looking for him?"

"Of course we have, but so far they have drawn a blank. However, something might happen at any moment. We never know out here what is going on until it is right under our noses."

"I know just what you mean, Robert, but I want everything possible you can give me to tell the Prime Minister when I return."

"I will have a fully detailed report ready for you and I sincerely hope that Warde will turn up and tell you more than I am capable of doing."

"I hope so too, if only for his daughter's sake – "

Lord Lytton looked at him quizzically.

"She is very lovely," he said. "Are you in love with her, Charles?"

Lord Kenington smiled and shook his head.

"I know what you are expecting me to say and the answer is 'no'. I have no intention of getting married. I like being a bachelor and 'playing the field', if that's not too vulgar a word for it."

"But you have done that for a long time and you know as well as I do, Charles, that you have to provide an heir."

"If you talk exactly like my mother, I will leave immediately for home!" Lord Kenington said. "I will then tell Disraeli that you are far too frivolous to cope with anything serious out here in India!"

"If you are not careful," Lord Lytton answered, "I will throw the inkpot at you and that will spoil that very smart suit of yours!"

"Be careful of it," Lord Kenington protested. "It's the only really decent one I possess and I put it on in your honour!"

They were both laughing, having known each for a long time and, although Lord Lytton was older, they still behaved rather like schoolboys when they were together.

"I am now going to have a swim," Lord Kenington announced, "and I was rather hoping you might join me."

"I have too much work to do," Lord Lytton replied. "It is impossible for anyone at home to realise how much is written down in India. It will all no doubt delight our grandchildren, while I find it extremely irksome."

"I am not going to be sorry for you, Robert   You know, as well as I do, that you have been a huge success so far and everyone is saying that you are the best Viceroy India has ever had."

Lord Lytton looked a little embarrassed.

"Do they really say that?" he asked.

"As if you did not know," Lord Kenington replied. "You are brilliant in every way and I am told that eyebrows are raised here because of your rather bold redecoration of the ballroom."

"That is true," Lord Lytton laughed.

"I am further told," Lord Kenington went on, "that the Japanese wallpaper that used to be here has disappeared to some fine pictures brought from Knebworth, your house in Hertfordshire."

"That is also true. I expect you have also heard too that now the walls clash horribly with the scarlet of the Officers' coats!

"Yes, I have heard that too!"

"Then they will just have to put up with it," Lord Lytton said. "Anything is better than shabby rooms, which they become more quickly in India than anywhere else."

"I agree with you, Robert, but you can understand it was considered quite serious news by the Cabinet."

"It would be, but then the silly fools should have something better to talk about."

They both laughed and Lord Kenington added,

"I will want better information than that and I am anxious to know what you are keeping from me and I shall want, as Warde is not available, to talk to some of the other top men in *The Great Game*. I have a note here of their names, which Disraeli gave me the day before I left home."

"Let me see it," the Viceroy said and held out his hand.

Lord Kenington gave it to him and Lord Lytton read it slowly and then he exclaimed,

"Two of these men are dead! One has resigned and, as you know, Warde has at the moment vanished."

"What about the other two, Robert?"

"They are in Calcutta, as far as I know and you will have to wait until you go back before you can meet them."

"Then what you are really saying," Lord Kenington said, "is that there is no one in Simla for me to talk to about *The Great Game*, who will tell me anything that I do not know already."

"There are a lot of minor people in it here, but they will only know the particular little parts they play and will certainly not have anything new to tell you."

Lord Kenington sighed.

He thought that, if this was indeed true, his journey had been a waste of time.

He rose to his feet.

"I am going swimming," he said, "and, if you must keep working, try to think of some way you can help me. I will feel a fool if I go home empty-handed."

As he spoke, an equerry entered the room.

After glancing at Lord Kenington, he walked up to the writing desk.

"Major Harold Warde is here, my Lord, and asks if you can see him."

CHAPTER SIX

For a moment there was astonished silence.

Then, as a man came through the door, the Viceroy jumped to his feet.

"Warde!" he cried. "I am so delighted to see you."

He walked to the Major and held out his hand and as he did so Lord Kenington also rose.

"We have been desperately worried about you," the Viceroy was saying. "Now you turn up and I cannot tell you how glad I am that you are here."

"I am very glad to be here myself," Major Warde said. "But you will understand why I was detained when I tell you what has happened."

The Viceroy remembered that he had a visitor and turned towards Lord Kenington.

"I want you first of all to meet Lord Kenington who has come from England to discover for the Prime Minister a little more about *The Great Game*."

The Major turned and held out his hand to Lord Kenington, who was surprised to see that he was wearing uniform.

He had thought if he did come back, he would still be in some disguise, but instead he was shaved and smartly turned out.

"I am delighted to meet you," Lord Kenington said.

"And you must be grateful to Lord Kenington," the Viceroy chimed in, "because he has brought your daughter here from Calcutta."

The Major's eyes brightened.

"Aisha is here!" he exclaimed. "That is excellent news. I had thought she would still be waiting for me in Calcutta."

"She would have been," Lord Lytton explained, "except that Lord Kenington was wise enough, as he was coming here, to bring her with him."

Before Major Warde could speak, he added,

"Now please sit down and tell us exactly why you disappeared and why you left us worrying about you."

"I am sorry about that," Major Warde said, "but I think you will understand when I report to you that quite by accident I discovered that the Russians were planning an attack on a Fort on the North-West Frontier."

"A Russian attack!" Lord Lytton exclaimed.

Major Warde nodded.

"They had worked up the local tribesmen and, when they were least expected, they intended to rush the Fort and set it on fire."

The Viceroy drew in his breath.

"As bad as that," he muttered.

"I have been thinking, like you, that it would not have been successful, but I had to warn the Garrison and I only arrived there a day before the onslaught was planned."

"And you prevented them from carrying it out?"

"The Garrison did so very effectively by firing their guns, as if they were practising, in the direction of the frontier. The noise they made and the fact that the Fort was seen to be so active deterred the Russians from doing what they planned."

"I think it was brilliant of you, Warde."

"This is just the sort of story I want for the Prime Minister," Lord Kenington said, "and it will confirm the answer to his question as to whether we need more troops in India than we have at present."

"Of course we need more," Major Warde replied. "I have said so a number of times, but no one will listen to me. Perhaps they will now."

He did not sound very optimistic about it, but the Viceroy said,

"Lord Kenington will make it very clear that more troops are wanted. Also that *The Great Game*, to which we are eternally grateful, is surely living up to its reputation."

Major Warde smiled.

"No one could have done more than you have," the Viceroy went on, "and, as you well know, when you retire, you will be acclaimed as we dare not do yet."

"I think it is something that you will be able to do very soon," Major Warde said quietly. "Too many people were well aware, when I reached the Fort, that I was the conveyor of the news that sent the Garrison immediately into action."

"Do you mean," Lord Kenington asked, "that you cannot go on in *The Great Game*?"

"Not if I wish to survive. There was no time for pretending to be anything but the conveyor of the warning that they were to be attacked. The stupidest recruit knew I was the only one who could have brought such a message when they had not had a visitor for several weeks."

"Well, it's a really wonderful way to bring down the curtain," the Viceroy said, "and I can only thank you from the bottom of my heart."

"You will have to do more than that, my Lord," Major Warde replied. "I have been asked by Colonel Brewhurst to get reinforcements sent at once and to convey to the powers that be exactly what occurred."

"What I am longing to know," the Viceroy said, "is how you discovered the plot in the first place."

"In the usual way," Major Warde replied lightly, "by listening and, because I was suspicious – which is why I came up here – that something was going to happen. I had no idea that the Forts on the North-West Frontier are sure to be the first target for anyone who intends to invade India."

"So you think the Russians are really serious?"

"They are little more than twenty miles away from us at present," Major Warde said quietly.

"As near as that!" the Viceroy exclaimed.

"Not in great force at the moment, but if they see open gates, so to speak, right in front of them, they will undoubtedly move in."

It was now Lord Kenington's turn to gasp and he enquired,

"You really think that is possible?"

"It is what they are aiming to do and everyone who works in *The Great Game* will tell you it has been in the forefront of their minds since the Cossacks started causing havoc in Asia. Behind them come the troops and guns."

"Do you think they will be at all upset or shall we say alarmed that this plan to destroy the Fort was foiled?" the Viceroy asked.

"It was planned, but it did not take place. However, as Colonel Brewhurst and I have ascertained, there were a number of men we thought were Russian soldiers mixed up with the tribesmen. When they all withdrew, we could see them more clearly and there were certainly a considerable number of them."

He paused for a moment before he went on,

"When our men search their hiding-places, which they had started to do when I left, they will undoubtedly find a great store of arms, besides, of course, the materials with which they intended to set fire to the Fort."

"I can only thank you on behalf of Great Britain for saving us from losing that particular Fort."

"I repeat what Colonel Brewhurst has asked me," the Major answered, "to urge you to send him more men and more guns as quickly as possible."

"Which of course we will do," the Viceroy replied.

Major Warde now turned towards Lord Kenington.

"Is Aisha really here?" he asked. "If she is, I must thank you most sincerely for looking after her."

"When you were not on the quay at Calcutta to meet her," Lord Kenington said, "I took her at once to Government House, where we learnt that you were missing and they were very concerned about you."

Major Warde made a helpless gesture.

"It was just impossible for me to communicate with anyone while I was making for the North-West Frontier Fort. I could only hope that Aisha, who is a very sensible girl, would go to Government House and ask for me."

"That is exactly what she did, only I went with her. I don't expect you know that she had to travel alone and I had the privilege of taking care of her."

"Travelled alone!" Major Warde now exclaimed in astonishment. "What happened to the Dean and his wife?"

"The Dean was taken ill at the last moment and it's not necessary for me to say that I saw at once that your daughter was far too pretty to travel alone without getting into trouble."

He saw the expression on Major Warde's face and added quickly,

"But I was able to help her and, of course, when I learnt that she was your daughter, it was something I was only too willing and anxious to do."

"Then I am extremely grateful, my Lord. I had no idea that Aisha would be travelling alone."

"There were a few difficult moments, but I am sure she will tell you about them."

"As you can imagine," the Major said, "I am very anxious to see her."

"Of course you must be," the Viceroy said, as he rang a silver bell on his desk. "Later you must tell Lord Kenington all that he wants to know and I am more curious than usual to discover that you have again succeeded so magnificently, as you invariably do."

Major Warde smiled as an equerry opened the door.

"Ask Miss Aisha Warde to come immediately," he said, "but don't tell her who my visitor is."

"Very good, my Lord," the Equerry replied.

He closed the door and the Viceroy said,

"It is very important that no one in this house party should realise why you have been delayed."

"It was usual Regimental duties," the Major replied.

Lord Kenington laughed and said,

"You should have said, 'very unusual ones'!"

"If they have to be the last," Major Warde said, "I could not have had a better end to the drama. When the guns flared out just as it was getting dark and the tribesmen and the Russians began to run, it was so like a melodrama. I could not for the moment believe it was real."

"They were waiting in hiding until dark?

"Behind every bush, in the long grass and in holes they had dug in the ground," the Major replied.

"I know the Prime Minister will be delighted by the story and it will make the Liberals, who are continually saying that we are exaggerating the situation, look foolish."

"You should ask them to come out here for a short time," Major Warde suggested. "They would soon learn the truth!"

"That is exactly what I want to take back with me."

At that moment the door opened and Aisha, looking very attractive, walked in.

"You wanted me, my Lord?" she asked.

Then she saw her father.

"Papa!"

It was a cry of sheer unabridged joy, as she ran across the room and threw herself against him.

"You are back! Oh Papa! I have been so worried."

"I know you have, my dearest, but you might have guessed that I would turn up like a bad penny!"

"You have come back and that is all that matters," Aisha said. "I have prayed and prayed you would be safe."

"And your prayers have been answered," Major Warde smiled.

He was holding his daughter very close to him and he kissed her again and again before he said,

"I told you not to worry and now you will never need to do so again, because we are going home."

"You are coming back to England?" Aisha gasped.

"I am retiring and there will be no more sleepless nights or worry about your poor father."

"Oh Papa! That is so wonderful! Nothing matters except that you are not lost, as I thought you were."

"Thank God I am here and alive," he sighed.

"I tell you what you ought to do now," the Viceroy remarked, "and that is to go into the garden for a short while with your daughter. Then, if you will, come back here, Warde. I want to hear your story step by step so that Kenington can take it to the Prime Minister."

"I think to be honest, my Lord," Major Warde said. "I will tell him what I think he ought to know. And seeing that for the moment I am still in *The Great Game*, there are certain matters on which my lips are sealed."

"Of course, of course," the Viceroy agreed. "We appreciate that and will not, I promise, press you."

"Come along, Papa," Aisha urged. "There is so much I want to tell you about what is happening at home and how thrilled I am to see you."

She slipped her arm through her father's and drew him towards the door and, as he reached it, the Major turned back towards the Viceroy.

"As you see, my Lord, families come first and duty second and that in my opinion is exactly as it should be."

"Indeed," Lord Lytton agreed. "And who could resist such a charming and beautiful member of a family as you have?"

As the door closed behind them, the Viceroy gave a deep sigh.

"I have never been so grateful in my life," he said. "I thought for certain something had happened to Warde. As it is, now that he feels he must retire, I cannot think how we will manage without him."

"There are a number of other men in *The Great Game*," Lord Kenington pointed out.

"I am very well aware of that," Lord Lytton replied. "Equally I have always liked Warde more than any of them and we will miss him more than I can say. But, if he wants to go, you can be quite sure he has a good reason for it."

In the garden Aisha took her father to the seat near the swimming pool, the coolest place she had found.

"Oh, Papa, I am so pleased to see you!" she sighed. "I have been terrified ever since I arrived that something dreadful had happened to you."

"Don't let's talk about it, dearest, just tell me what is happening at home and how you managed to come here on your own. It was something I would not have allowed if I had known about it."

Aisha told him what had happened on board the P & O Liner and how she had wisely asked Lord Kenington if she could be seen talking to him and how he had been extremely kind and then had rescued her from the awful Arthur Watkins.

The Major was listening attentively, but she knew he was angry that such horrors should have happened to her simply because she was alone.

"You should have waited, dearest, until the Dean was better," he said finally.

"I so much wanted to see you, Papa, and it is such wonderful news that you are coming back to England and I will never be alone again."

"I will see to it, but we will have to find ourselves a house in London. I understand that the Prime Minister wants me to help him on India and, if a hint is to be believed, I am to be a Member of the House of Lords."

"I have been told that, Papa, and no one deserves it more than you."

They talked until it was time for luncheon and then they went into the reception room to be introduced to the rest of the house party.

They were all delighted to meet the newcomer.

At the same time Aisha kept thinking that they eyed her father curiously and perhaps it would prove dangerous to him if they had the slightest idea of who he actually was.

After luncheon was over, the Major said to Aisha,

"I have to see the Viceroy some time and I think he would like me to go to his study now."

"Why can I not come with you?" Aisha asked.

"Because, my darling, even you are not supposed to know the innermost secrets of *The Great Game*, which, of course, is what the Viceroy wants me to give him."

"And will you, Papa?"

The Major laughed.

"Just as much as is good for him and the same will apply to your protector, Lord Kenington."

"He was extremely kind to me and I could not have managed the voyage if he had not been there."

"It's a journey you should not have made."

"I would have gone round the world a hundred times to see you, Papa. I could not have stayed at home and thought about you waiting for me on the quayside at Calcutta."

"Which I was unable to do anyway."

"Tell me what happened?" Aisha begged him.

Her father shook his head.

"It's over and done with. Now I only want to think what we will do when we reach London and where we will find ourselves a nice house that is not too far from the War Office."

"I hoped I would have you all to myself," Aisha sighed. "But they will make you work and work and I will be lucky if you come home for dinner."

"Nonsense! I have done the work that I was really good at. Although I will help the Prime Minister when necessary and the Secretary of State for Foreign Affairs, I have every intention that you and I will enjoy ourselves, especially you."

"By going to parties? You know, Papa, I would much rather talk to you and indeed to Lord Kenington. I am not interested in young men who have not even crossed the English Channel or are obsessed with horse racing until they can think and talk of nothing else."

"You cannot be a cynic at your age, my dear. You have to try to enjoy life in a thousand different ways before you finally find the path that suits you best."

"Now you are preaching to me. I will only listen to you, Papa, if you tell me the things I want to know and not the things I should know."

Her father laughed.

"I promise you that we will spend as much time as possible together before we return to Calcutta, which will be tomorrow or the day after. But I must go to the Viceroy now."

"Very well, Papa, I will go and sit where we were this morning and count the minutes until you join me."

"I should think it will take a thousand of them," her father replied.

Then he kissed her and walked away.

"Come and watch us play polo," one of the young men called out as he saw her standing alone.

"It's too hot," Aisha called back.

"I will find you a cool place to sit in," he persisted, "and I am longing to show off how well I can play."

"I still say it's too hot on the polo ground and I like being here," she replied. "The garden is so beautiful and it's quite cool by the swimming pool."

"Now you are tempting me," the young ma

"But I promised to play and therefore I have to leave ⌐

"I expect I will still be here when you come bac.
Aisha said lightly.

"Well, we are going to dance this evening and I book myself here and now for the first dance and for a great number of others too."

"I will put it down on my card," Aisha smiled.

He walked away and she turned to the swimming pool.

She had only gone a short way when an elderly woman who had been at luncheon came walking up to her.

"I am very anxious, Miss Warde," she began, "for you to tell me about your father. Every time I mention him, people seem reluctant to tell me anything about him. As he is so good-looking and distinguished, I am curious."

"I believe Papa has a very good reputation as an Officer," Aisha replied.

"I think it is more than that. Someone whispered to me that he is in the Secret Service."

Aisha managed to laugh.

"You must not believe all you hear. Papa has done so many things in his life that I think they make up stories about him as if he was a hero in a novel. But I assure you that his heart is with his Regiment and he greatly enjoys being a soldier."

"I am quite certain it's more than that," the lady persisted.

Then much to Aisha's relief, they were joined by two young men looking for the elderly woman.

"We are going to play tennis, Aunt Lucy," they said, "and we would love you to come and watch us. Nicholas is a particularly good tennis player, so I am bound to be beaten."

"...ld enjoy that very much," the lady replied. "...e with us, Miss Warde? I am longing to go ...l about your father and I am sure, as he is ...ere are marvellous stories for me to hear

"I am afraid you would find them very dull," Aisha said, "because, if you think about it, all Regimental service is much the same. Papa has been very lucky to be serving in India where he has so many friends and, unlike most people, he does not mind the climate."

The tennis players had walked ahead and the lady lowered her voice before she said,

"Oh, do be kind and tell me more about him. I can see you are keeping it to yourself and I am intrigued."

Aisha wanted to say, 'and I suspect, very talkative.'

But she merely replied,

"You will have to ask Papa. I don't suppose he will be very long with the Viceroy. He will be in the drawing room at teatime."

The elderly woman gave a sigh of exasperation and walked away without saying any more.

Aisha was sure she was one of those busy-bodies who wanted to know all about celebrities so that she could convince her friends that she knew everything there was to know about everybody.

'She is just like the Countess of Dartwood,' Aisha told herself, 'and thank goodness they've not arrived yet.'

She thought with any luck that she and her father would have left before they came and she was quite certain that the Countess, if she had the slightest suspicion of what her father had been doing, would chatter about it – or if it was sensational enough, would shout it from the roof-tops.

'The sooner we get back to England,' she thought, 'the better. Then Papa will be free from *The Great Game*, and from the kind of people who suspect something must be happening if they have not been told all about it and therefore they are tiresomely inquisitive.'

She walked away alone to the swimming pool.

As she did so, she was saying a heartfelt prayer of thankfulness that her father was safe and now she could be with him alone as she wanted to be.

'No one has done more than he has for England,' she mused, 'and now he will be able to enjoy himself.'

It was still impossible not to feel the shadow of danger and she had been acutely aware of it ever since she had arrived at Peterhof.

However reassuring both the Viceroy and Lord Kenington had been, she knew instinctively that they were extremely worried about her father.

They had only pretended to be confident because they did not want her to feel as alarmed as they did.

'Now we will go home,' she thought, 'and I will persuade Papa to stay at our house in the country until the summer is over. Then, if he has to go to London, we will find a nice little house near the river and there will be no more ears listening at keyholes or a feeling of apprehension every time the door opens.'

When she reached the swimming pool, she was pleased to see that there was no one else there and she sat down in the seat under the trees.

'I do hope that Papa will not be long,' she said to herself. 'I have so much more I want to say to him.'

*

In the Viceroy's sitting room, Major Warde was telling him and Lord Kenington exactly what he believed were the weak spots in the defences of India and what additional forces and equipment he thought necessary.

The Viceroy was writing it all down, whilst Lord Kenington knew his own memory was the safest place in which to store the secret information he was hearing.

He then asked several questions that the Viceroy thought were extremely intelligent.

Major Warde was able to answer them with copious information and reasons that would undoubtedly support the Prime Minister against the Opposition.

They talked for nearly an hour and then the Viceroy sat back in his seat and said,

"All I can say to you, Warde, is that you have been brilliant, not only in what you have done but in what you have planned for the future. I only wish you would stay here and organise it."

"It is always wise to know when one should close the door and pull down the curtain," the Major replied. "As you are aware, my Lord, there are several very weak spots in our defence and I am quite certain Lord Kenington will explain these when he returns to London."

"I know how grateful the Prime Minister will be to you," Lord Kenington said. "At the same time everything will be pooh-poohed and talked down by the Opposition."

"I suppose really that is what they are there for," the Viceroy replied. "If you ask me, if we did not have a competent Opposition, we would not have even half the resources we have at the moment."

"That is a paradox but true," Major Warde said. "When I think how difficult it has been to get anything from England in the past, I am grateful, very grateful, for even what we have at present."

"Yet you will want more," Lord Kenington added.

"That might be said of everything in life. If one was completely content with things as they are, we would sink into an apathy that would undoubtedly end in disaster both for ourselves and for the nation."

He spoke in a way that made Lord Kenington think of Aisha – it was the way she had talked when she sounded more like an elderly politician than a young and pretty girl.

Her father was an exceptionally good-looking man and Lord Kenington could only understand that Aisha had inherited from him not only her beauty but a part of his brain and his superb powers of perception and imagination.

"I am extremely interested in all that you have said today," the Viceroy said to the Major. "I only hope when you return to England that you will speak out your views and not keep them to yourself."

"I am retiring into private life, my Lord."

The Viceroy laughed.

"I very much doubt it. You know, as well as I do, it will drive you mad to see people doing things the wrong way and perhaps undoing everything you have created."

The Major made a gesture with his hands, but the Viceroy went on,

"If you ask me, you are someone who will go on fighting until the last breath. But only when you are dead and buried will they realise how great you really are."

"I am very grateful for those few kind words, my Lord. It is always wise in life to know when enough is enough. Those who cling onto their careers when they are really finished are usually laughed at."

"I am sure that is something people will never do where you are concerned," Lord Kenington said. "When the Prime Minister hears what I have to say, it will merely confirm his thinking that you are the most outstanding and resourceful man who ever fought for India."

"If I stay here listening to you any longer, I will become conceited," Major Warde sighed.

He rose to his feet and said to the Viceroy,

"I know you will allow me to leave you, so that I can be with my daughter."

"Of course," the Viceroy agreed, "and thank you again for all you have told us."

Major Warde left the room, but Lord Kenington did not accompany him.

He waited until the door was shut and then he said,

"I suppose the sooner I go back to London and talk to Disraeli, the more you will feel at ease, Robert."

"I am certainly very perturbed by what Warde has told us," the Viceroy replied. "I suspected things were bad, but not as bad as they apparently are."

He gave a deep sigh before he continued,

"Thank God he uncovered the plot before the Fort was set alight. I only hope we can keep it from becoming news. Otherwise there will undoubtedly be those who will panic and expect the same to happen wherever they are."

"You know Warde will not talk," Lord Kenington replied, "and at this time of the year there are very few visitors to the North-West Frontier."

"That is true. Even so I am wondering from where I can move even as little as a Battalion without it being obvious that something is up."

"I should wait," Lord Kenington suggested, "until all signs of the threatened disaster have disappeared and that includes Russians who have already withdrawn."

"That is good advice and I will certainly consider it, but you must admit, Charles, that things are happening in India that make me extremely anxious. And it is appalling to think that the Russians are very much nearer than the authorities at home believe."

"Nevertheless it would be just impossible without a very large force indeed for them to take over India," Lord Kenington said. "But we might have to fight to preserve it, and that would definitely mean many more men than we have at the moment."

"I agree with you and I will leave you to make very clear to the Prime Minister about the urgency of sending us reinforcements immediately. I believe also we are short of long-range guns."

"Make a list for me," Lord Kenington proposed, "and I will leave as soon as you want me to, Robert."

"I have no wish for you to leave as soon as you have arrived," the Viceroy answered. "You know, Charles, how much I enjoy having you here. It is delightful having someone to talk to who is intelligent and who knows as much as you do."

He gave a deep sigh before he added,

"If you only knew the idiots I have to put up with, who talk as if they know everything about India, but in actuality know nothing!"

Lord Kenington smiled.

"Perhaps it's a good thing that they know as little as they do. Otherwise they might panic and you have no wish to cope with that."

"No wish at all. To be truthful I like my peace and quiet with just a few of my old friends to talk to."

There was little point, Lord Kenington thought, in saying that he sympathised with the Viceroy.

Having endless parties at Peterhof, because it was traditional, was exhausting and naturally everyone of any significance who came to India expected to be a guest of Lord Lytton.

He was just about to make his friend laugh, when the door opened.

An equerry said,

"Major Warde wants to see you, my Lord, and he said it is very urgent."

"Yes, of course, show him in," the Viceroy replied.

Then he looked at Lord Kenington and said in a lower tone,

"What on earth is going to happen now? Warde said he wanted to be with his daughter."

Then the door opened and Major Warde entered.

There was an expression on his face as he walked straight across the room to the Viceroy that made Lord Kenington stare at him.

"What is the matter, Warde?" he asked.

There was a pause.

With some difficulty he managed to reply,

"They have taken Aisha and left this on the seat where she was sitting."

As he spoke, he handed the Viceroy a crumpled and rather dirty piece of paper.

On it was written in badly spelt Urdu,

"Give us the names of 17, 24, 85 and 96 or your daughter dies."

CHAPTER SEVEN

Lord Kenington stared over the Viceroy's shoulder and, when he read what was written, he exclaimed,

"It cannot be possible! What have they done with her?"

"They have taken her away," Major Warde replied. "They will lock her up, so that she will starve to death if I don't do as they have demanded."

"What can we do then?" the Viceroy now enquired. "You know as well as I do they will murder those four men when they know their names."

There was no need to explain to Lord Kenington that everyone in *The Great Game* was known by a number. They never gave their real names to anyone when they were on a mission.

It was exceptional, as in the case of someone as important as Major Warde, for anyone to know who they actually were.

"How could this have happened in my garden?" the Viceroy asked.

"Very easily I am afraid, my Lord, as, although you are not aware of it, there is a spy amongst your servants. I must have been followed, although I was certain that I was clear of them and they have learnt that my daughter is here with me."

"I suppose that Aisha was sitting by the swimming pool?" Lord Kenington asked.

"That is where I said I would meet her when I left you," Major Warde replied.

He walked across the room and stood with his back to them while he looked out into the garden.

Then he came back to the desk and said,

"I must do everything possible to find her quickly. But I would like, if possible, someone to come with me."

"I will come with you," Lord Kenington offered at once.

Major Warde looked at him.

"Are you sure? I don't need to tell you it will be extremely dangerous and you may lose your life."

"I could not stand by idle and allow Aisha to die in such a ghastly way and I promise to do everything you tell me if I may accompany you."

"But have you any idea where to go?" the Viceroy asked the Major.

He was staring at the piece of paper and wondering how in the tranquillity and quiet of his garden this outrage could have happened.

"I am almost certain," Major Warde said after a little pause, "that I know where they will take her."

The Viceroy looked up.

"Tell me," he said, "so that at least I will have some idea where you have gone."

Major Warde bent forward and spoke a word in Urdu that was just a whisper and the Viceroy stared at him.

"*The Mountain of Eyes*?"

Major Warde nodded.

"I think so. That is where they took Lord Swinton, who you remember disappeared and was never found."

"I have often wondered what happened to him," the Viceroy said. "Although we had many people searching the whole of India for him, they never found him."

"That is where he was taken," Major Warde said still in a low voice, "and he died of starvation."

"You found him?" the Viceroy asked.

Major Warde nodded.

"And you never told anyone!"

Major Warde made a gesture with his hands.

"What was the point? As he was dead, I did not want our enemies to know that we had been astute enough to find where they had taken and murdered him."

"I see your point. Do you really think they will have taken Aisha there?"

"It is nearer to here in their territory than anywhere else, but with the number of soldiers guarding you, there should have been no trouble."

"The sentries should have seen anyone entering the garden," the Viceroy said angrily. "I will find out how this could have occurred."

"Not until I have found Aisha," Major Warde said firmly.

"Do you mean that?"

"I mean that we must behave outwardly from this moment as if nothing has happened."

Major Warde was still talking in a very low voice. It could not be heard even on the other side of the room, let alone by anyone listening outside it.

He looked round and pulled up a chair to sit beside Lord Lytton who was still at his desk and, without saying anything, Lord Kenington did the same.

"Kenington and I," Major Warde said, "will leave after luncheon. We will tell everyone we are going to look at a new gun that has just been taken on by the Regiment. As you know, there is a small detachment of them about ten miles from here."

The Viceroy nodded.

"Actually we will drive on to an address I have no intention of telling you. There we will change and make our way on foot to the place I have just mentioned. That name must never be spoken and it is best if you don't even know it exists."

"I understand. Is there anything you require?"

"I have enough money of my own and I now have a companion to accompany me and who will carry on if by chance the enemy disposes of me."

He paused for a moment while the two men stared at him and then he added,

"I think it is unlikely, as long as they believe that I am giving them what they demand."

"It is the most unforgivable blackmail I have ever heard," the Viceroy fumed. "To me it is utterly appalling. But, as I have always been told, no one is ever safe in this country from our enemies."

Major Warde rose to his feet.

"I am going to circulate with your guests," he said, "as if nothing has happened and Lord Kenington should do the same. When we are not here for dinner this evening, you can tell them that you have had a message to say we have met some friends while visiting the Regiment and that you understand we will not be back until tomorrow."

"I can only pray that at least is the truth," and then the Viceroy added in a kindly voice,

"You have had a very nasty shock, Warde. Let me get you a drink."

The Major shook his head.

"I need my brain to be very clear and then with the help of God I hope to find Aisha."

"I suppose there is no question of an arrangement with them, such as paying for Aisha?" Lord Kenington asked.

"If this is planned by who I think it is, they have plenty of men behind them and what they really want is to eliminate as many as possible of those in *The Great Game*. The numbers they have given me all belong to the bravest and most successful of our members and they may have been waiting for a long time to find out who they are. But, now because I am here with my daughter, we have played right into their hands."

"Then we have to rescue her, we *have* to," Lord Kenington insisted.

"The only chance we have is that the people who are blackmailing me have no idea that I know how poor Swinton died. His bones are still lying where they left them and the mystery of his disappearance is still talked about by his friends and the men who worked with him."

Lord Kenington was musing that no one in England realised the strength and the power of Russia's spies. They had infiltrated deep into India and were causing trouble wherever they could.

Their main objective at present was to deal with the Forts and loyal tribes on the North-West Frontier. These could delay and hinder their advance, even though there was no question of winning against a strong Russian Army.

The fact that distinguished men like Lord Swinton could disappear and his body never found was a factor that would strengthen the resolve of the Prime Minister.

He was already convinced that even more help was needed in India than it was currently receiving and it was appalling that a young girl like Aisha could be kidnapped from the Viceroy's garden without anyone knowing.

'We *have* to find her,' Lord Kenington murmured again to himself.

The Major rose to his feet.

"I am going now," he said, "to watch the tennis or the polo and appear completely unconcerned, as if nothing unusual is happening. If I am asked where Aisha is, and you should ask me openly over luncheon, I will reply that she has a headache and is lying down."

"What about the servants?" Lord Kenington asked quickly.

"I have already thought of that. I am going up to Aisha's room now and, if the servants are outside, they will hear me talking to her. Then I will come out and say she has a very bad headache and does not wish to be disturbed. I will lock the door and take away the key."

"You think of everything," the Viceroy remarked.

"This is a moment, my Lord, when none of us can afford to make a mistake," Major Warde replied quietly. "If we do, my daughter will die and I expect I will die too."

"You must not talk like that. I cannot believe that you and Charles together will not succeed in finding her and bringing her back here."

"Believe that and it will help us."

He walked across the room and opened the door.

"I promised to go and look at the tennis players and I will see you at luncheon."

With that he closed the door quietly behind him.

For a moment there was a hushed silence between the Viceroy and Lord Kenington.

Then the Viceroy said, putting his fingers up to his forehead,

"I cannot believe this is happening. I have always been assured that I am over-protected. Yet a girl has been taken out of my garden without anyone noticing it."

"It makes me furious too," Lord Kenington said, "but for the moment you must not ask questions of anyone. If Warde can act his part well, so must we."

"You are quite right, Charles, but it makes me so angry that this should happen to one of the best men who has ever worked for us and to his charming daughter."

"I know, but she has the same courage as her father and I feel confident that we will find her."

He was thinking as he spoke how Aisha and he had talked about the Tibetan monks and how she was interested in the way they could communicate with each other.

'Perhaps,' he thought, 'she will try to tell me where she is.'

Then he told himself he was being over-optimistic. It was ridiculous to think that a young girl could have the same powers that the monks in Tibet had worked at all their lives to achieve.

Yet it was there in his mind and he kept thinking of it all the time over luncheon, trying to make conversation with the guests and hearing the Major not only talking but laughing at the other end of the table.

'He is a magnificent actor,' he told himself.

At the same time he knew that the Major had had a great deal of experience. He was determined that no one staying in Peterhof should know of Aisha's disappearance.

The luncheon seemed to drag on and take hours, but it was actually no longer than the day before.

When it finished, the Major said in a loud voice,

"Are you ready, Charles? It's going to be a hot drive, but I promise a cool drink when we reach camp."

"Where are you going?" a woman guest asked.

It was the same lady who had been so curious with Aisha earlier in the day.

"We are going to a detachment of my Regiment," the Major said. "We have a new gun that has recently arrived from England and I now wish to show it to Lord Kenington. In my opinion it is one of the most effective weapons to have been developed for some time."

"How interesting," the lady twittered.

This was a splendid titbit of gossip that she would be able to convey to her friends.

"Do tell me all about it, Major."

"I will tell you about it tonight, but now we must be on our way. I have already told the Viceroy what I think about his roads and it was not particularly complimentary!"

Everyone laughed and those who were going out to play tennis said,

"Well, good luck and we expect we will be a lot hotter on the tennis court than you will be on the roads."

"I will test that tomorrow by having a game with you," the Major countered.

"I shall look forward the challenge," was the reply.

*

The Major had already changed from his uniform into a casual thin suit and Lord Kenington did the same.

There was an open carriage drawn by one horse waiting for them outside. There was only room for two people to sit in it, so that it was obvious that they would not be accompanied by the groom.

"Don't worry if we are delayed," Major Warde said to him in Urdu. "We might, if there is a party this evening, stay tonight at the camp and the horses will be well looked after."

The groom bowed and the Major drove off.

The horse was pretty fast and they covered quite a distance before Lord Kenington asked,

"How far is this mountain?"

"It is not really a mountain, but it is remote and at one time inhabited by Holy men who worshipped some peculiar God of their own. They were therefore found a place where no one would interfere with them."

"Go on," Lord Kenington urged.

"Well, these Holy men then dug small caves into the mountainside, each one for himself and there were a great number of them. Long after they moved on the caves have remained. Some of them extend some way back into the mountain and it's difficult to go into them because of falling rocks."

"And you are sure they have taken Aisha there?"

"No one can be sure of anything, but I have been told that our enemies use these caves and it was there that I found the body of Lord Swinton."

He paused for a moment and then added,

"It was, of course, only his skeleton, as he had been missing for over five years, but his signet ring was still on his finger bone and I recognised the Swinton crest."

"But you did not report it?"

"What was the point? He had been missing for so long and it was more or less accepted that he had died after falling into a lake or perhaps some mountain torrent."

"And no one found him except you, Major?"

"There was no way of knowing it was he, except by the ring, which is now in my possession. I was told some months ago that our enemies had used those holes in the hillside when they needed to hide or, as on this occasion, they had a prisoner, but it was only a casual suggestion and there was no actual proof that they were doing any harm."

"I understand that, if you had talked, we should not be going there now," Lord Kenington commented.

"Exactly, but I find that in life and, as you know, my life has been very peculiar, the strangest coincidences do happen when we least expect them. Thinking it over, I cannot imagine anywhere else near Peterhof where Aisha could be hidden."

"Do you really believe that if you told them the names they want, they would let her go?"

"That is a question I cannot answer for sure," Major Warde replied, "but quite frankly I don't think they would. I have had experience of them in so many ways. A number of their activists have been shot or imprisoned by us and they would obviously be delighted to torture me."

Lord Kenington drew in his breath.

"You don't think that it would be wise to bring some soldiers to search every hole in the mountain, which we may not be able to do ourselves?"

"If they did find Aisha, she would be dead," the Major replied.

There was no answer to that and Lord Kenington remained silent.

The road improved in places and was very rough in others and eventually they reached a village in which there was a Church, some fairly well-built houses and a number of smaller places of habitation.

It was at the foot of a range of small hills that were not high enough to be called mountains.

Lord Kenington had not spoken for some time and, almost as if he asked the question, the Major said,

"This village has living in it a very interesting man whose vast collection of ancient weapons and implements, which have been found in the hills, is famous. He also purveys a great deal of rubbish in his shop that he sells to tourists. He is much respected in this part of the country."

The way he spoke, rather than what he said, told Lord Kenington that this was where they had someone to assist them.

The Major drove the horse into a yard at the back of the shop and a man came out and went to the horse's head. The Major talked to him in Urdu and he was obviously pleased to see him.

Then, as he took the horse away, the Major and Lord Kenington entered the back of the house.

The passages were very narrow and the walls very old and the Major led the way and Lord Kenington found himself in what he imagined was part of the shop.

There were many strange and ancient uniforms and some weapons, that could only have been used a hundred years earlier, hanging from the ceiling.

They had been there a minute or two when from the front came a man, middle-aged, but with a somewhat bent and contorted body.

He held out his hand in delight to the Major and they chatted together for a moment in Urdu before Lord Kenington was introduced.

Then he found himself looking into the weird eyes of the man, who he was quite certain was scrutinising him.

It was almost as if he looked, not so much at his outward appearance, but into his very soul.

Then, as if he was reassured, his eyes flickered and he said to the Major,

"You'll find everything you want upstairs."

"Thank you, you never fail me," the Major replied, "and this time what I am doing is absolutely vital."

The man smiled.

"It always is," he muttered and disappeared the way he had come.

The Major opened a door that had been hidden by the display of ancient uniforms and inside there were steps leading up to the floor above.

The ceiling was low and they had to bend their heads.

The Major opened another door and they entered a small square room where there was only one very narrow window that was covered up so that it would be impossible for anyone to see in from the outside.

When Lord Kenington looked round, he realised why they were there.

Hanging on the wall and on several chairs were clothes and one look at them told him they were the sort of clothes used by members of *The Great Game* to disguise themselves.

Without speaking, the Major began to search for some for Lord Kenington.

Around half-an-hour later two ordinary and rather ugly men left the shop by a different route from the one they had entered by.

They slipped out at the back of the shop, but this time they turned to the left.

Passing over a piece of rough ground, they walked up a road that soon trailed off into nothing but a path.

Still the Major went on.

They walked in silence, looking, Lord Kenington thought, so shabby that no one, even their own mothers, would have recognised them.

He had touched up his face with a cream that gave him the same complexion as an Indian and the Major's was darker still.

In fact looking at him Lord Kenington knew that he would have passed him on the road and not imagined for a moment who he really was.

The clothes he himself was wearing were exactly what might have been worn by any of the men who worked on the roads.

They saw no one and they were now walking over the rocky ground of the lower part of the hills above them.

Without speaking, they carried on and on for what Lord Kenington felt must be miles and yet it might have been less because it was impossible to move at all quickly.

Then, as the sun began to sink, it became far cooler and not so unbearably hot as it had been when they started.

Next, when Lord Kenington almost felt that they were walking to nowhere, he saw a strange valley ahead.

On each side of it rose what he knew was called by the natives *The Mountain with Eyes*.

The hills, and it was something of a compliment to call them mountains, were not really high, but they were extremely rocky.

Cut into the rock on either side of the small valley there were dark holes – they looked like the entrances to caves or, as the local people called them, 'the eyes of the mountain.'

He could understand that it would have been a perfect place for any religious sect to settle. They would be near to each other and, running through the valley, was a small stream.

It was then to his relief that the Major, who had walked a little ahead, sat down on a convenient rock and

Lord Kenington, who was beginning to find that his legs were tiring, sat down beside him.

"We are here," Major Warde said, "but we have to wait until dark before we can go any further."

The place he had chosen for them to sit down was concealed by a rock overhanging them.

"Do you think there is anyone there?" he asked.

The Major shrugged his shoulders.

"One never knows," he said. "There might be no one or possibly a number of people. It all depends on who is using the place at the moment."

"How are we to know where they may have hidden Aisha?" Lord Kenington enquired.

"That is exactly why I wanted someone with me," the Major replied. "There will be just time for us to search every hole and corner of this place. You take one side and I will take the other."

Lord Kenington drew in his breath.

There were very many holes in the rock face and, if he was to search them in the dark, he felt there would be every danger of slipping and injuring himself.

Then he realised that the Major was opening what looked like a small sack, which he had carried with him all the way. Because he thought it was a weapon of some sort and they were walking in silence, Lord Kenington had not asked him what the sack contained.

Now he saw that the Major was drawing out of it two lamps of the sort that workmen use and contained only a candle inside them.

But, because they were used in this part of the world, Lord Kenington realised that they would throw enough light for one to see down the passage to a cave and inside it.

"I have brought us three extra candles each," the Major said, "in case we need them. We can only pray that one of us will find Aisha quickly."

"Yes, of course we must," Lord Kenington agreed.

He could not help feeling that, if they did not find her quickly, it would take a very long time to reach the far end of the valley if they were to investigate every cave.

"Now what we have to do," the Major said, "is to rest and to concentrate mentally on what lies before us."

He smiled before he added,

"It is what I always do before I set out on a difficult and dangerous mission and I most sincerely believe that I have been successful so many times because I use not only my brain when I am working but also my heart."

Lord Kenington looked at him in surprise.

"I don't understand, Major."

"I want to win. I believe I will win. And with the help of God, I do win."

It was the sort of thing that Lord Kenington had not expected a man like the Major to say, but he respected him for it.

It suddenly occurred to him it was more or less exactly what Aisha had said the monks did when they were getting in touch with a man miles away from them.

'If I think about her, perhaps I will find her,' Lord Kenington said to himself.

He glanced at the Major and realised that his eyes were closed. He was not only concentrating on what he was about to do but was also relaxing completely.

'I must do the same,' he determined.

Then, as he too closed his eyes, he felt that Aisha was calling him.

He told himself at first it was just his imagination.

Then he was sure that she was thinking of him.

Just as he had been able to read her thoughts and she had read his, they were for a moment linked with each other spiritually, although physically they were apart.

When he opened his eyes, he found that the sun was sinking in the West. Darkness was coming quickly, as it always did in India.

Now it was hard to see clearly below them and the far end of the valley was in deep shadow.

"Now we can move," the Major said unexpectedly. "You must not light your lamp until you are actually in a cave. And be very careful to blow it out before you come outside."

Lord Kenington looked at him in surprise and he explained,

"If anyone is here and sees a light moving about, they will of course investigate. And if they suspect it to be intruders, they will shoot at us.

"So what you have to do is to light your lamp when you are far enough into the cave to be certain it will not be seen from the outside. Then hold it as high as you can until you have gone in deep enough to make sure that there is no one there."

Lord Kenington thought it would take a very long time, but he did not comment and then, almost as if he had asked the question, the Major said,

"There is a full moon tonight and in a short while it will be easy to see your way from cave to cave, although I need not ask you to walk very carefully."

As they were talking, the sun seemed to disappear except for a luminescence in the sky and overhead the first stars were appearing.

"Now we will go," the Major said. "Do you want the caves on the right or the left?"

For a moment Lord Kenington did not reply.

Then, as if he felt once again that Aisha was calling him, he said,

"I will take the right. If I find Aisha, how do I get in touch with you?"

"I think you will find that, if we shout, our voices will echo in a strange and almost frightening way. Those who hear us at this time of the night, unless they are very civilised, will attribute it to the demons or the ghosts who are supposed to haunt these caverns. They will therefore run as quickly as they can in the opposite direction!"

Lord Kenington laughed, but by putting up his hand he prevented himself from making a sound.

"I understand," he said, "and I will take the right."

"Very well and I will take the left. Let me know if you find Aisha and you had better take this with you."

He drew from under his coat a very long shining stiletto. It was much longer than an ordinary one and was almost like a small sword.

Lord Kenington, who had seen one before, knew that they were one of the most dangerous weapons for any man to encounter.

"If there is anyone in any cave at the moment," the Major said, "they will certainly be an enemy and are better dead than alive. They will, I am sure, have the same sort of weapon or perhaps a pistol. It is up to you to move first and very quickly, if you wish to save your own life."

"I understand," Lord Kenington nodded grimly.

"I am glad, very glad indeed, that I have you with me," the Major said. "Good hunting and you appreciate that to me everything depends on finding my daughter."

There was an emotional note in his voice that Lord Kenington found very touching, but he merely replied,

"And good hunting to you," before he started to climb towards the right side of *The Mountain with Eyes*.

It was very difficult to gain a firm foothold in the gathering darkness and Lord Kenington did not hurry.

He was trying to feel that Aisha was calling him. It seemed to come and go.

When it was with him, he was almost certain it was her voice reaching out to him.

He entered the first cave and once inside as far as he could go, he then lit his lantern.

The cave was empty and it was impossible to go any further.

He wasted more no time there, but went outside and climbed once again as carefully as he could to the next one.

After he had explored five caves with no result, he found himself wondering if he should have taken the left side of the valley.

He could not see any movement, but he was certain that the Major was moving quicker than he was.

'At this rate I will be doing this for the next two or three months!' he thought as he set off again.

He entered the sixth cave and was suddenly aware, as he moved into it, that at the far end there was a light.

As it could not be the Major, he instinctively pulled out his stiletto and waited for whoever was holding the lantern to come towards him.

Even as he did so, he thought that once again Aisha was calling to him.

Then, almost before he was ready, the light came much nearer.

He could see that it was carried by a man who was undoubtedly no ordinary Indian.

Lord Kenington was standing with his back to the wall of the passage and, as the man approached him, he moved forward to confront him.

Even as he did so, he saw the man raising his right hand and there was a pistol in it.

Obeying the Major's instructions, Lord Kenington moved swiftly forward and drove his stiletto with all his strength into the man's heart.

He gave out a strange guttural sound and fell over backwards.

Lord Kenington knew that he must be dead.

His lantern, still alight, had fallen beside him and Lord Kenington took it from his hand.

Then, as he looked down to make sure that the man was dead, he pulled the stiletto out of his breast.

Stepping over the prostrate body, he walked down the passage.

The lantern was as good as his and Lord Kenington was able to see his way down a very much longer passage than he had found in the other caves he had checked.

On and on he went and now he was almost certain that he would find Aisha at the end.

Quite suddenly the passage seemed to open into a small cave.

It was then he saw at one side of it that Aisha was lying against the wall, her arms and legs tied fast with a rope that prevented her from moving.

She was very pale and her eyes were closed and for one frightening moment he thought that she was dead.

Then, as he moved towards her, her eyes opened.

As he said her name, she gave a cry that seemed to echo and re-echo round the cave.

"You have come, you have come!"

Lord Kenington knelt down beside her and said in a voice that did not sound like his own,

"I have found you, Aisha! I heard you calling me."

"I was calling and calling for you to come and save me and now you are here," she cried. "How is it possible you have been – so clever as to find me?"

Her voice was jerky and almost incoherent.

Then Lord Kenington said,

"You are safe now and your father is with me."

Then, as if he could not help it, he bent forward and his lips found hers.

For a moment they were both very still.

Hardly realising what he was doing, he put down the lantern and put his arm round her neck.

"I have found you," he breathed, "and it is the most wonderful thing I have ever done in my whole life. I found you after your call of love."

He kissed her again.

A long kiss, because it seemed to bring them closer to each other even though the rope was between them.

Then Lord Kenington asked,

"They have not hurt you?"

"No, I am all right, but please take this rope from me, it is very tight round my legs," Aisha managed to say.

It was easy for him to undo it and then, as her arms were now free, she could slip it down onto the ground.

Almost instinctively she put her arms round him.

"You came, you found me," she sighed with a little sob, "when I thought I would die here."

"That is what they meant you to do, but you might have known that your father would save you."

Then, because it seemed as if he could not restrain himself, he was kissing her again, kissing her until they were both breathless.

At last, as if he came back to reality, he said,

"We must get out of here in case there are any more of them."

"There were more until it was dark," Aisha said, "and then they went away to find something to eat, leaving only one man to guard me."

"And that man is dead."

"You killed him?" she asked.

He nodded.

"How can you have been so clever as to find me?"

"I will tell you all about it," Lord Kenington said. "But first let me get this rope clear of your ankles."

He pulled it away and then lifted her to her feet.

She seemed so small and so fragile he could hardly believe it was possible that she had been through so much.

It must have been incredibly frightening for her.

As if she was reading his thoughts, she said,

"I was very very frightened, but I prayed that you and Papa would come to me. I thought if I sent out my cry for help, as the monks do, that you would hear it."

"I heard it and by a miracle it brought me to you."

She smiled up at him and she looked so lovely in the flickering light that he kissed her again.

"I knew when they came and told me that you were missing," he declared, "that I loved you."

"And I loved you when you saved me on the ship, but I did not know that what I was feeling was love – "

"You must tell me all about it later, but first we must get out of this place and tell your father you are safe."

The passage was so narrow that they had to walk in single file. Lord Kenington went first carrying the lantern high so that it would be easy for Aisha to follow him.

Only when they came to the dead man did he stop.

Lord Kenington stood with his back to him and made Aisha squeeze past towards the entrance to the cave.

"Don't look!" he urged. "Just look straight ahead. I am right behind you."

He realised as he spoke that he had left his stiletto behind and then he thought it would not matter if the Major came quickly in reply to his call.

Outside the moon was high, casting a silver light over the valley and making the scene exquisitely beautiful.

As if she needed his protection, Aisha had moved close and was clinging to him.

He put his arm round her, then bent and kissed her forehead.

"I love you, Aisha, and I will tell you how much when we have reached safety."

He thought as he spoke that perhaps there would be other men who might attack them and that he had been a fool to leave his stiletto behind.

Then he knew that somehow he must attract the Major and he must do what he had told him to do.

He shouted and, as his voice rang out, it echoed and re-echoed down the valley.

To his relief it was only a few moments later that he saw a lantern on the other side of the valley and he knew that it was carried by Major Warde.

Because he thought it would be a mistake to make any more noise, he waved his arm and Aisha waved too.

Then he helped her back the way he had come.

Past the five caves he had examined, until they then reached the place where he and the Major had rested.

Lord Kenington put his arms round Aisha again and sighed,

"You led me to you and now I will never lose you again."

"I was frightened, very frightened," she whispered. "When they took me away and brought me here, I thought that you and Papa would never find me."

"But you knew we would try."

Then, as her father was approaching, he kissed her again, thinking that there would be time for words later on.

"You have found her! You have found her!" the Major exclaimed, as he clambered up to where they were.

"I knew that you would try to rescue me, Papa, but I was so afraid that you would not know of this strange place."

"It was your father who was brilliant enough to remember this was where they had kept a prisoner before," Lord Kenington said.

He realised as he spoke that the Major was almost past saying anything because he was so overjoyed to see his daughter again.

There were tears in his eyes as he asserted,

"My dearest, this will never happen to you again. I am taking you back to England and that is where we will stay."

Aisha did not answer.

Lord Kenington thought that there would be plenty of time later to explain that Aisha now was his and he was determined not to lose her.

She knew what he was thinking and then he felt her hand creep into his.

As his fingers closed over it, he knew they were not two people but one and even their thoughts were known to each other.

It would have been a long walk back to the shop where they had come from, but fortunately the Major knew that there was a farmer not far below them who he was sure had a horse and cart.

The man was at first rather suspicious, but when the Major offered him a considerable sum of money to drive them back to the village, he agreed with delight and then hastily put his horse between the shafts.

It was not a particularly comfortable way to travel and Aisha sat between the two men.

Her father held one hand and Lord Kenington the other.

The shopkeeper was delighted to see them and even more delighted with the money he received for the clothing he had lent them.

"You know, sir," he said to the Major, "I'm always ready to give you what you wants when you wants it."

"We have always relied on you and you have never failed us," the Major said, as he gave the man double what he expected.

Although it was unnecessary, Lord Kenington also gave him a considerable sum.

Then they were driving back to Peterhof in their own carriage.

"You must tell me exactly how you were clever enough to find me, Papa," Aisha asked as they drove on.

"At the moment I am concentrating on getting us back to a civilised meal and a comfortable bed," the Major answered. "Then it is essential that we leave at dawn or as early as the Viceroy can organise a special train for us to travel on to Calcutta."

"Do you think that is necessary?" Lord Kenington asked.

"Completely and absolutely necessary. If there is one thing these people who kidnapped Aisha dislike it is being deprived of their prey and of being thwarted in their intentions."

He paused before he added,

"They are obviously aware that I was responsible for frustrating their attack on the Fort and I am a marked man. But, as I would like to live a little longer, I must leave India immediately and so must Aisha."

"And I am coming with you," Lord Kenington said. "I have everything I need for the Prime Minister and the sooner I take it to him the better."

"Not only for the Prime Minister's sake but for your own," the Major remarked.

Aisha gave a little cry,

"Oh, please, please be careful."

"Are you really thinking of us, when you have been through so much?" Lord Kenington asked.

She smiled up at him.

"Of course I am. You are the only two men who matter to me in the whole world. In fact you are my world. As I thought I would never see either of you again, I am saying a prayer of thankfulness with every breath I draw."

"I knew that you would pray we would find you."

"Of course I did. I prayed from the moment they threw something over my head and held it so tight that I could not scream and carried me away, lifting me over the wall and then tied me up so that I could not move."

"You are not to think about it," Lord Kenington said. "As you can imagine, the Viceroy is furious that the sentries did not prevent you from being taken away in that appalling fashion."

"I am sure that the Viceroy is not guarded strictly enough," Aisha reflected.

"And it is something they will have to think about now this has happened," the Major said.

Because there was nothing on the roads at that hour of night, it did not take them long to reach Peterhof.

They were, of course, stopped by the sentries at the gate, who were astonished to see who was in the cart.

They hurriedly let them pass.

It was after midnight, but, when they drew up at the front door, they were told that the Viceroy was still in his room and would naturally wish to see them.

"We would all like something to eat and drink," Lord Kenington said as they walked down the passage.

When a servant opened the door, they saw that the Viceroy was sitting at his desk and he looked up almost as if he disliked being disturbed.

When he saw who it was, he gave a cry of delight.

"You have found her!" he exclaimed.

"Yes, we have found her, but only her father could have been clever enough to guess where she was hidden."

"They have not hurt you?" he asked Aisha.

"I am so very very thankful to be free. I thought I would die, but Papa and Lord Kenington were brilliant enough to save me."

"I want to be told all about it," the Viceroy said. "But first I am sure that you are hungry and thirsty."

"I have already presumed to tell your servants when we came in that was what we required," Lord Kenington said. "I am sure Aisha must be even hungrier that we are."

"I have had nothing to eat or drink since luncheon," she said. "But I was too scared to think of anything except – that I was going – to die."

Because there was a heartfelt sob in her voice, Lord Kenington reached out towards her hand.

As he smiled at her, the Viceroy said,

"Have we something to celebrate, Charles, besides Aisha's return?"

"I was hoping, after your rebukes, that you would congratulate me because I am going to be married," Lord Kenington answered.

"That is the best news I have heard for years!" the Viceroy exclaimed.

Then, as he looked from one to the other, the Major enquired,

"Are you saying what I think you are saying?"

"Oh, yes, Papa!" Aisha cried. "I love Charles! I loved him when we were on the ship, but I did not realise it was love. I just wanted to be with him and I was so disappointed when we had to come here, because I really wanted to be alone with him."

"I suppose I can understand that," the Viceroy said. "At the same time, Charles, I am delighted and I know you could not have found a more beautiful bride or a brighter one if you searched the whole wide world."

"I have been aware of that myself ever since I was foolish enough to let her land in this country, which is full of danger and from where we are running away as quickly as we can," Lord Kenington replied.

The Viceroy laughed.

"I have never known you talk of being frightened before. But naturally what has happened means that you will have to leave as quickly as I can arrange it."

"I thought you would understand that," the Major said. "Not only am I marked, but so is my daughter and so is Lord Kenington."

"I assure you," the Viceroy replied, "you will have every possible protection to speed you home safely. And I will immediately arrange for you to travel in my private train to Calcutta."

"I shall enjoy that," the Major murmured.

"And also," the Viceroy continued, "for you to be taken to England by *H.M.S. Victorious* which is in port at the moment."

"An Ironclad – how exciting!" Aisha cried.

"I thought it would please you."

"You have forgotten one thing," Lord Kenington said.

"What is that?" the Viceroy quizzed him.

"H.M.S. Victorious would give us a delightful if unusual honeymoon, but I think that we should be married first!"

"Of course!" the Viceroy agreed. "And, as I intend to be your Best Man, Charles, you can be married here in my Private Chapel before anyone else is awake."

Aisha and Lord Kenington looked at each other.

"That will be wonderful," she whispered.

A servant brought in food and the Viceroy insisted on drinking their health in champagne.

"My throat is so dry that this is a joy," Aisha said. "Usually I don't particularly like champagne."

"It is the right thing for you to drink at this moment to celebrate our engagement, short though it may be," Lord Kenington said, "but his Lordship is correct, the sooner we leave this country the better and I think that you should have some sleep after all you have been through."

When they went upstairs, Aisha found her bedroom and Lord Kenington looked in the room next door.

"This room is empty," he said, "and this is where I am going to sleep tonight."

"I think actually it is something I should do," the Major answered, "but, as my room is on this corridor only a little way down, I will allow you to begin immediately being Aisha's personal protector!"

"I am very grateful, Major, because if I was far away, I would find it impossible to sleep for worrying that she would fly out of the window before I could prevent it!"

"I am not going to fly anywhere, but stay with both of you and it will be lovely if we all go home together, so that I can talk to the two men whose conversation I really find enthralling."

"We can talk tomorrow," her father said. "Now I am going to bed, but first I am going to thank God that you are safe and unharmed. I know that in itself is a miracle."

"I am going to thank God too," Lord Kenington came in, "not only because I will have the most beautiful and adorable wife any man has ever been lucky enough to find, but also an extremely distinguished and clever father-in-law."

They all laughed and Aisha added,

"And I am the luckiest girl in the world because I have you both."

She kissed her father and then, as he tactfully went to his room, she held out her arms to Lord Kenington.

"I love and adore you," he sighed, as he drew her close to him. "I love you until I find it impossible to find words to tell you how much."

"When did you first know you loved me?"

"I think I loved you from the very first moment you came to me for help. But I was so determined not to be married and to remain a bachelor that I would not listen to my own heart."

"Now you have listened, what does it tell you?"

"That I have found someone I love more than I thought it possible to love anyone. She is part of me, just as I am part of her and that is why together we make one complete person."

Then he was kissing her, kissing her wildly.

And Aisha was kissing him back determinedly and with a passion she had never known before.

"I love you, I love you," she cried.

She went on saying it even after he had left her and she crept into bed.

She knew, as she did so, that she had found the love she had always wanted, but thought existed only in books.

Or perhaps in the minds of those who lived in the mystical world of Tibet and other parts of India.

It was the love that she knew was Divine and which everyone sought but few were privileged to find.

It was the love that came from God.

When two people were joined together as she and Lord Kenington were, their love would grow until they were, as he had said, not two people but one.

When they married, the Gates of Heaven would be open to them.

"I love him. I adore him," Aisha whispered before she fell asleep.

In the next room Lord Kenington was saying as he tossed from side to side,

"I love her, I love her! How can I be so lucky as to find the one woman in the world who was made for me and is already a part of me?"